FAE OR FAE KNOT

FAE OR FAE KNOT

PROVIDENCE PARANORMAL COLLEGE BOOK TEN

D.R. PERRY

LMBPN Publishing
PMB 196, 2540 South Maryland Pkwy
Las Vegas, NV 89109

Version 2.1 November 2022
ebook ISBN: 978-1-64971-943-0
Print ISBN: 978-1-64971-944-7

CHAPTER ONE

Gemma

"There is no bright side to losing my kid." I snarled at the woman on the other side of the desk, jutting my chin forward to show her my tusks. "But you wouldn't know anything about that, would you?"

"Gemma!" My grandfather pressed one hand down on my shoulder, keeping me in my chair. To someone of his generation, tossing the Headmistress's infertility on the table as a caltrop was way out of line. But I'd never been one to stay inside those.

If he hadn't stopped me, I might have leaped over that mahogany expanse and gotten right in Henrietta Thurston's face. Adding some injury to insult was something I hadn't done in too long. There was nothing like losing all contact with my daughter to bring back the old rage that had fueled my mosh-pit inhabiting youth.

"You're correct, Miss Tolland." The Headmistress leaned forward in her chair, keeping her gaze locked on mine. Two white-tipped tails peeked out on either side of her straight back. If I'd pissed her off with the infertility comment, it didn't show. "I shouldn't have implied that your loss gives you time to study. Instead, I should have said accepting my third offer of a full scholarship here at Providence Paranormal College will help you learn more about how to navigate the other side of faerie law. You'll need that knowledge now."

"Why are you doing this?" I crossed my arms, winding my hands around my elbows and digging in with my nails so hard I broke skin. The other two people in that room smelled it, even though I healed in seconds. Being a Troll had powerful benefits.

"When I see potential, I want it at my school." The Headmistress's smile showed more teeth this time than it had seven years ago when she'd given the same reason for her first offer. That made sense. She hadn't been a Kitsune then.

"I'd say my King already recognized that."

"Yes. He's wise and I'm sure you've learned much while rising to the rank of captain in his navy. But other parts of your education are still lacking. I'm giving you the opportunity for a well-rounded perspective."

"What's the catch?"

"You're navigating in the shallows, girl." Grandpa tapped my arm with one of his massive elbows. "This is the last of the Thurstons you're addressing and the first Kitsune in mortal existence since our courts sundered."

"My family name is of no consequence, John." Henrietta Thurston's eyes glittered like sea glass. "But the magic and instincts that come with these tails is. My patience is not what it used to be." She looked at me, narrowing her gaze to a tight focus. "I'll make this offer one more time. Before I do, check your coincidence. It'll guide your course as surely as the stars."

I wasn't sure how she expected me to "check coincidence." That wasn't in a Troll's skill set, Seelie or Un. What did she mean? Considering the Headmistress had lived most of her life as an Air magus, probably something intellectual. I closed my eyes, wishing I could sift through memories with a touch, like Henry Baxter.

Three was a magic number for any faerie. This was the third time I'd sat in this office, getting an offer most people wouldn't refuse. Supposedly, Tony Gitano had taken the same full scholarship without even reading the fine print. The first time, I'd walked in just minutes after learning I was pregnant with Hope. The second time, it had been hours after the king had saddled me with a captain's commission on Hope's third birthday. And now, it was one full day since my little girl took up the Alkonost's feather and went Seelie by accident.

All three had something in common—circumstances beyond my control. The bane of my life was being reactive, someone who had little choice but to make counterstrikes and do damage control. Even as a captain, I served alongside my grandpa the admiral, who had preempted me all these years. It was time to activate something for once.

If accepting a scholarship wasn't autonomy, nothing was.

"Yes. I'll take it."

"Excellent." The headmistress pulled a piece of paper from the top drawer of her desk, set it down, and pushed it across.

"Hmm." I skimmed all the words on the page, then blinked as I looked it over a second time. "There's a mistake here. It says I start coursework now, but it's Midterm."

"Yes." Thurston nodded. "You'll have a directed study with me for your general requirements, culminating in a CLEP exam this Friday to get you credit for life experience. I expect you to pass everything on the first try and gain enough credits to place at Junior level. After that, you will complete a half semester intensive on coincidence and contracts with Professor Watkins and some consultants I've hand-picked."

"You already tagged people in on this?"

"Yes. I believe in your potential that much, Miss Tolland and so do the educators I mentioned. Next semester, you will have a normal course load for a second semester Junior."

"Okay." I pulled a pen out of the cup on my side of the desk and scrawled out a signature.

Asking about catches hadn't been a bad idea. The huge one was starting with exams in five days. But I'd brave that. Confidence was one of my strengths. The other was devotion to my little girl. Vast as an ocean, it was. I'd weather this if it meant that someday I'd be able to see her again.

"Tenacity, thy name is Gemma."

"What was that?" The Headmistress's raised brow and crooked grin told me she knew full well my inside voice had escaped and heard what it said, too.

"Nothing." Instead of pouncing on the fact that she'd asked me a question, putting her a third of the way into my debt, I caved. With good reason. "Thanks for this opportunity, Headmistress." I stood up and extended my hand. Grandpa loomed behind me.

"Thanks for taking it, Miss Tolland."

We shook on the whole deal. Henrietta Thurston put her back to me, placing my contract into a folder inside a large filing cabinet, paneled to match her desk. She might have had a swanky office and everything, but at least the Headmistress filed her own paperwork. I respected that.

The last thing that caught my attention before trailing out of the room after my grandfather were Henrietta's tails. They waved like kelp at the bottom of the sea, serene as though testing currents I had no awareness of.

I'd just made a deal with a Kitsune, offered thrice, signed and shaken on.

If that wasn't trouble with a capital T, I didn't know what was.

Albert

I hate talking politics. Engaging in them boiled my blood. And I had a good reason for this particular nasty. But helping a family member get settled with a peer came before having to explain myself to my Queen.

"I can totally climb that tree." My daughter pouted.

"I'm sure it's well within the scope of your abilities, Hope." I took a breath, and she discarded the rest of my explanation like a duce in a game of War.

"The way you talk stinks like yesterday's fish." Her nose wrinkled, exactly the way her mother's used to back in our Trout Academy days. I couldn't help but love her instantly, too.

"This is how the queen's folk learn to speak." I tilted my head, knowing my phrasing and tone of voice would do nothing to soften my next words to her. "You're also one of hers, so eventually you'll also talk this way."

"You get it from your mom." Hope wrinkled her nose as she remembered our brief meeting with my mother. "She's even worse." She rolled her eyes. "God."

"No divinity there, just another duchess of the queen's court." I held my tongue about watching her language. For an almost-six-year-old with such a large vocabulary, learning to cuss while growing up surrounded by literal drunken sailors is unsurprising. I was lucky she hadn't called me a scurvy knave yet. "You must stay here for a year and a day, like any newcomer to either faerie court."

"But I don't like it here." Hope blew a raspberry.

"The laws of fae magic don't change based on our feelings." I glanced down at the top of her head, framed by the rainbow wings she'd sprouted upon becoming the Alkonost. "The queen needs that time to prove your loyalty, especially considering you are one of the three mystic birds."

"That sucks." Her tiny fists clenched as her wings drew closer to her back. "I hate this."

"You're entitled to that opinion as long as you follow the queen's rules."

This time, Hope didn't bother using her words to answer. Instead, she growled, teeth bared to show off her elongated bicuspids. I sighed and shook my head. The queen's treacherous consort had robbed her of her destiny by flinging a magical feather talisman at her. But there was no bringing back her genetic or magical predisposition at this point.

"Climbing that tree looks like the only fun in this entire place. There'd better be a good reason I'm not allowed to do it." She tapped her foot, gazing up at me as she displayed her skill at avoiding direct questions.

At least she understood how fae debt worked. Hope's distaste for wordiness and over-explaining was sure to be the first of many hurdles I faced over the course of our new journey together as parent and child. I erred on the side of brevity.

"Because it's special."

"So what?" She shrugged. "I'm special, too."

Unsure what to say, I paused. I couldn't say the tree was more special than her because I knew in my heart that if it came down to Hope or the arboreal wonder, I'd choose her in a heartbeat. Declaring it off limits for good would be an outright lie. Honest and direct weren't Sidhe staples. Fred Redford would explain it better but he was trying to rescue Bianca Brighton. I'd have to do my best imitation of good old fashioned Redcap bluntness.

"This tree's special differently than you are, Hope. It's where the power our ranks convey comes from and climbing it now is out of the question."

"Oh." She stared down at her feet as we continued along.

"I know you're bored, but that'll change soon enough." I reached out, hand hovering a few inches from the top of her head. But I didn't have the courage to face her reaction to any sign of affection. The first time I'd tried it, her eyes had gone watery as she called for her mother through trembling lips. I refrained, letting my hand drop back to my side as though defeated by an army of thousands.

"I'm not playing with anything like Grandma's clockwork dolls again." She shook her head, ruddy bobbed hair flying out in a nearly perfect circle. "They're creepy."

"No dolls, I promise. But you will have fun."

"No idea what it is, then." She stopped walking and peered up at me.

"Not a what, a who." I smiled down. She narrowed her eyes. "Ed Redford is coming to visit his brother. He'll be bored, too."

"I don't want to play with a little kid."

"He's older than you by about two years."

"And probably just some kind of lame Changeling."

"No. He's the youngest medium in Rhode Island. And he's waiting to meet you right on the other side of the courtyard."

"Medium?" She bounced on her toes. "That means he sees dead people! Woah, cool!"

Hope took off running through the courtyard. I lengthened my stride to keep up but let her have a respectable distance. Growing up half-time on an Unseelie Pirate ship had done no damage to Hope's sense of wonder, even if it gave said sense a macabre twist. I had to be honest with myself. Her excitement at meeting a child who must have had a near-death experience before he got out of diapers would have made me cringe if she hadn't been my daughter.

But I couldn't show her how disturbed I was. I owed her and her mother for all the missed years. Fred had tried to convince me that my absentee fatherhood wasn't my fault. He'd failed. Fault or no, honor bound me. I'd be as good a father as possible or die trying. But with the way my life had gone so far, the latter was far likelier.

Ed

I hit the flagstones and covered the back of my neck with my hands. In the Under, I never knew whether any person running toward me was friend or foe. I knew my shifters though, so I thought she was dangerous. Half-open wings equals bird body language for 'fight club.'

"Um, kid."

I didn't dare look up, but already knew which ghost had spoken, anyway. The not-quite Spanish accent gave her away.

"Go away, Kasa."

"No. Anyway, it's just another kid."

"Huh?" I blinked, even though the only thing in front of my face were the shimmery flagstones the queen liked so much.

"She's some kind of weird bird kid, but not much different from you."

"Oh." I knew of her, even though we hadn't met yet. Al's daughter.

I stood and brushed shiny grit off my knees just in time almost to knock the bird girl over. She fluttered her wings and hopped backward before my head clonked her on the chin.

"I'm Hope Tolland. Or it might be Dunstable, I dunno." The girl tilted her head to one side, making her unevenly chopped red hair fall far enough to brush the top of her wing. "You're my size." She blinked. "Are you sure you're older than me?"

"Well, yeah." I rubbed my hand on the back of my head. "Mama says my growth got stunted."

"Okay." Hope Tolland grinned, then folded her hands in front of her.

"You praying or something?"

"Nah. Just a way to chill my hands out." The grin countered her hands by unfolding into a smile.

"Excited isn't how most people act when they see me." I kicked at a tiny stone.

"Yeah, but you're a medium, so that means you can see all the ghosts here, too." She jerked her chin at the one over my shoulder. "Hi!" One of Hope's wings flapped in a waving gesture.

"Hello, little bird." Kasa's voice sailed over my head like an annoying fly.

"Thought I told you to leave, Kasa."

"Oh, no!" Hope pouted. "It's cool finally to be able to see ghosts. Don't send her away. Please?"

At first, I thought Hope was acting, but the glassy shine in her eyes and the red on her face changed my mind. The girl's happiness reminded me of a glass when you pour hot chocolate into it by accident, about to crack at any second because it couldn't take the heat.

"Fine." I shrugged. "Kasa can stay, even if she's the most annoying coyote shifter ever to go ghostly."

Hope set her hands free and clapped. Her smile was more like hot chocolate in a mug this time. It belonged.

"Mama always used to give the five-cent tour of her ship to newcomers. Are you gonna give me one for this place?"

"As much as I can, I guess." I glanced to my left, at the passageway I still hadn't taken time to explore. "This place is humongous, though. I don't know more than about a half a penny's worth."

"You talk like the knight." She jerked her thumb back over her shoulder at Sir Albert Dunstable.

"Um, that's your dad." I never called my father "the duke" instead of "Dad."

"I guess." Hope shrugged. "Only met him a little while ago."

"Okay." I couldn't imagine not knowing either of my parents. But then again, Josh, the Alpha of the Tinfoil Hat pack, sent me here to find out stuff about Hope. Telling him that this girl felt alone and separated from her family might be important. It'd be even better if she'd tell me more. "Let's go see the stuff I do know. It won't take too long, so after that we can check out some things I didn't want to see alone."

"Cool!" Hope bounced, those rainbow wings fluttering but not enough to lift her off the ground.

"Hey, can you fly with those?"

"Nah, not yet." She shook her head. "Well, I haven't tried yet. But the knight says I shouldn't fly around in the queen's castle without her permission, anyway."

I glanced back over her shoulder where her dad stood. It was hard to think of Sir Al as someone's father, especially to a kid just a year and change younger than me. He wasn't much older than my brother, Fred. Al's eyebrows scrunched close together, which meant that her calling him "the knight" instead of dad bothered him. But I couldn't help with that.

"Well, let's go." The grin I tried to give her only covered half of my mouth.

To make up for being a sour apple, I gave her my hand. I missed my dad, Mama, too. Dad could visit any time, but Mama was locked up without bail. Her last ghostly partner made her do awful things and I wouldn't see her for years.

Hope was in the same boat with me, except her mom had done nothing wrong. When Richard Hopewell threw down something shiny, Hope Tolland had pounced on it without thinking. I would have, too, though it wouldn't have affected me. Because she got born in the Under and her aunt was a bird shifter, Hope had bonded with the thing, turned into a Seelie creature. Her mom was Unseelie.

The poor girl could look at her mother, maybe talk to her on the phone. The Faerie queen and king had split up ages ago, and now the fae courts had to be separated. Even a handshake'd get a faerie executed. At least the mortal laws allowed family visits complete with hugs when the kids got taken away.

I turned my head as we walked, watching Hope's bright hair and brighter wings bob along just ahead of me. Kasa had spent weeks whispering about all the guilt and sadness behind the smiles in this castle. And in that moment, my mission from Josh turned personal.

I had to help Hope Tolland. Maybe if I did, if I was honestly kind and good to her in her hour of need, someone would reach out and help me, too, in mine.

CHAPTER TWO

Albert

I let the kids go, pacing down the hall at a distance that gave them privacy while I could still see them. Maintaining tactful distances was second-nature for me, to the point where coming within an arm's length of most people got my nerves humming like live wires. This distance was freer for me, easier, more my speed. Until the voice came from somewhere near my shoulder.

"Who knew we had parenthood in common, Sir Knight," the voice purred. I recognized that rusty-nails-on-satin voice.

"Lady Harcourt." I nodded even though I knew she wouldn't pass or even pace me. Newport's dragon lady liked keeping most people off-guard, even her own son. But I knew plenty about overbearing mothers, even if mine hadn't stabbed her husband in the heart like Hertha had done to Wilfred. "What brings you to the queen's demesne?"

"You must have gotten the invitation, too." A rustle of thick parchment met my ears.

Sidhe hearing was second to none, even better than a vampire's. This had its drawbacks but for now it only announced the fancy card's presence in Hertha Harcourt's hand. A rasp of paper on metal meant she'd clutched it against the queen's amulet, which allowed her to remain in human form during her visits here.

"I'm afraid not."

"It's waiting for you at your round table seat." Hertha's chuckle sounded like an upended bottle of poison gurgling its contents into a world without antidotes, an apt analogy considering her dragonish magic type.

"I'll check there as soon as I am able, then." I jerked my chin toward my child and her playmate. The latter had a determined expression on his face as though their interaction carried an unusual gravity to it. "I've got to get them settled."

"In the nursery."

"Yes, that's where I was told to house them."

"So young Ed is also your charge. Sir Frederick must be on an errand."

"Something like that." Omitting Bianca's plight was easy. Ms. Harcourt couldn't be trusted even though her son, Blaine, was a more than occasional ally of mine.

"You probably won't ask me where I'm headed."

"I'd hardly dare to make any assumption about you or your plans, Lady Harcourt." While the title was honorary, using it couldn't hurt. The dragon lady was old and powerful in her own right.

"Good idea, Sir Knight. But you ought to know this. I've been charged with watching over the nursery while you knights and courtiers go about your business during these strange times. Your magical girl will be under my wing. The young medium, too."

We continued walking that way. The presence of a venomous dragon matron outside my field of vision should have caused a sense of dread or at least tweaking anxiety. Add in the fact that the woman in question had married two otherwise immortal dragons killed under violent circumstances, and I should have been quaking in my greaves.

Calm bobbed in the distance like an untethered buoy in a choppy sea. Fathers of small and impetuous children find little calm outside of sleep, even in newly discovered paternity. Peace was a land so distant, its presence lingered undiscovered on the furthest imaginable horizon. The last time I'd attained it utterly had been in Gemma's arms. I'd lived on the dull edge between misery and dread ever since my family dragged me before the queen and forced me to tithe Seelie.

The dragon at my back conveyed an unexpected sense of security. Hertha was so protective of her children, she'd killed to defend them. She'd slay me where I stood if it meant the kids stayed safe. I blinked, startled at the knowledge that I'd do much the same thing if our roles reversed.

"Did the queen give you this charge, Lady?"

"No, and I'm not at liberty to say who, either so don't ask again."

"Understood."

After a statement like that, Hertha probably expected me to burn internally with unabating curiosity. I didn't. Logic, deduction, and I had been close compatriots for most of my life and those old friends didn't fail me now. The way I saw it, three possibilities and one long shot existed.

The Goblin King. While the Harcourts seemed unconnected to the Unseelie monarch, Hertha or Blaine somehow getting indebted to him was not outside the realm of possibility. She hated the queen's suitor, Richard Hopewell, so she had little reason to get out of such a debt. But unless said favor was centuries old, I knew of nothing on record to imply one.

Headmistress Thurston. Henrietta's family, and the Harcourts went back as far as Rhode Island's Colonial days. Hertha had funded Phillip Thurston's westward oil-seeking expedition at the turn of the 20th century. She was also a Trustee at Providence

Paranormal College, with a dorm named after her late husband, Ignacius. The two ladies were long-time friends and their bond had likely grown stronger after Henrietta claimed her birthright as the first Kitsune to walk the earth in an age.

Finally, there was Delilah Redford, young Ed's mother. The senior medium awaited trial for the attempted murder of Professor Nate Watkins. Hertha's name was in the jail's visitor records on the day before we'd all ended up in this mess. Some of Delilah's ghosts had been precognitive in their living days, so they might have seen a situation where Ed would need a dragon's protection.

There'd been another name on that visitor log the same day: Joyce Watkins. I'd looked her up in the Registry because of the surname she shared with Delilah's would-be victim. She was in there, listed as a Psychic, type undetermined, flagged as missing. I'd filed the information away in case it mattered later. I had to include it in my ruminations.

Those ended as we reached the corridor's termination. A brightly colored door opened all on its own, the hinges creaking with the musical creepiness that porcelain dolls and monkeys in wind-up boxes shared.

Hope rushed in, Ed fast on her heels. I followed, but before I made it through the door Hertha brushed by me. I let her pass. A blanket-wrapped something or other rested in her arms, swaddled and cradled like the quietest baby in the history of this universe. For the record, the Under is eons older than the mortal realm.

Inside the queen's nursery, the first thing I noticed was the decor. Plush benches and alternating tables with rounded edges lined all the walls. Beneath each lay a nap cot. In the center, stretching between the floor and vaulted ceiling, was a replica of the tree outside. Magic hummed around it, and a quick inspection revealed magical wards that would slow and cushion any fall.

The tree had ample hand and footholds but also contained nooks for perching and resting, vines for swinging, and even cubbies stocked with toys and picture books. A trio of arched doorways stood to one side marked for girls, boys, and neither/either/or. I pictured a Sprite nursemaid and smiled. No such creature existed.

Hope

I charged the tree like it was Grandpa. Even he wasn't that big. That room and everything in it were the coolest things I'd seen since the feather I shouldn't have touched. My wings trailed out behind me like anime hands. They lifted my feet from the ground, too, and I changed my mind about the feather. I was meant to have wings, knew it in my bones, deeper than all Seven Seas stacked on top of each other.

Everything would have to work out somehow. I'd be with Mama again, Grandpa, too. It'd just take time. In the Under, faeries had lots of that. Kids like I used to be, kids like Ed, they still grew. My body would stay the same size here like Peter Pan's did in Neverland. Later, I could go back to the mortal world and get bigger. If I even wanted to.

The top of the tree was mine in ten seconds flat. Wings helped, but I'd forgotten about Ed's ghosts. Kasa gave him a boost, launching him up through the wards that only worked on the way down. He was like a whooping rocket, about to crash into me. I ducked.

"Quack!"

"Huh?" Ed hit the top branches face-first, getting a mouthful of magic leaves.

He spat them out, which was icky because of spit, not because he was a boy. Ed looked like one of those kids who washed his hands and brushed his teeth three whole times a day. No wonder someone as fussy as the queen didn't mind having him around. Ed was too neat and tidy.

"Yaah!" I reached out and mussed his hair on purpose, pulling it up between both hands the way Mama did when she put my hair in mohawks.

"Aaay!" He shook his hands at me, palms out. Of course. He was half Italian. "Not the hair!"

"'Kay." I shrugged and looked away from him. That meant down, right about where the poison dragon lady stood. My mouth dropped open, and I didn't even care whether any flies flew in.

The dragon lady had an egg. It was big as a boulder but I knew better because it looked like leather and had blue and green spots I'd never seen on rocks. It wasn't round like a turtle egg. Instead, it was an oval like eggs in the crocodile nest I'd found when Grandpa brought me to Disney World in Florida. The Captain Hook jokes I got to make were awesome. But anyway, I couldn't believe it.

"Ed, guess what?" I leaned in, hissing a whisper into his ear.

"What?" He tried patting his hair back down, but it was about as effective as an electric attack on a ground Pokemon.

"We're sharing a room with a real live dragon egg." I stopped myself from clapping my hands by pressing them together. "Can you believe it?"

"Yeah." Ed just shrugged.

"Why you gotta be like that?" I shook my head.

"It's just, I've already seen the newest Harcourt." He sighed, looking like meeting a baby dragon egg wasn't one of the coolest things in either world.

"Really?" I blinked.

"Yeah." He made one nod, like guys in action movies do.

"You think she'll let me get a closer look?" I twiddled my thumbs so he wouldn't notice how much I wanted to see the dragon egg.

"You want me to ask her?" Ed blinked, then held his hand in front of his face and butted his palm with his forehead.

"Hah! Three questions!" I clapped my hands, then rubbed them together. "You owe me!"

"Okay. If I ask her to let you say hi to the egg or whatever, will that get rid of the debt?" He frowned at his shoes. "Crap."

"Yup. Doodoo. Cacka. Poopie. Fewmets." I hardly ever talk about number two that much but frowning stinks more than dirty diapers and I wanted Ed to stop doing it.

Ed stared at me, then blinked. He shook his head, blinking again. His lips pressed together, tighter than my hands had before. And his cheeks got redder than the funny-smelling Mall Santa's breath. He wasn't going to laugh, or really, he wasn't going to let himself.

I reached out, goosing him under his arms. After that, he giggled himself straight out of the tree, taking me with him.

The magic wards slowed us down. We drifted like snowflakes even though I used my wings to make sure we landed on our feet instead of our butts. I felt like a shooting star or maybe a rainbow. If I'd made Ed Redford, the Mama's Boy laugh, I could do the same thing for my father someday.

But he'd left the room already, off on his errand to the stupid Queen. I settled into staying on the floor for now. It made sense, especially if I wanted to meet a baby dragon still in the egg. I'd make that sad knight smile someday, though. I had all the time in the Under.

CHAPTER THREE

Gemma

"Again."

Tails waved as the Headmistress of Providence Paranormal College clapped her hands. I let my eyes roll on their way up to peer at her. No one should sweat as much as I did that October. The fatigue that comes after running a marathon set its edge against my bones, mostly in my hips, though trying to work this magic hadn't engaged any muscles around them. Since my labor with Hope, I carried more pain there than any other part of my body.

"Tell me how you think I'll get a different result this time and I'll call you insane."

"Routine helps with spells like this, Gemma."

"I don't have time for habits. That's a thirty-day project, not a seven-day one."

"All the same, try it again."

"No. This is bullshit."

"Understood." She grinned. "But you signed a contract. Once more."

"Your contract and your CLEP intensive suck."

"Thank you for expressing your honest opinion. Pissing me off won't let you off this hook. Again."

The pit of anger that lived in my chest blossomed, fueling a growl that might have shamed a Great Dane. I opened my mouth to let the sound have its way, my sweaty hand gripping the length of wood in it so tight I thought it'd either crack under the pressure or eject.

A blast of air, frigid as the force behind Lake Effect snow, rippled out from the business end of the wand. Instead of going in a straight line as I'd expected, the cold went everywhere, even fanning out to slap me in the face.

Exhausted from the effort of generating that big a temperature change, I let the wand drop. The energy's absence didn't take away my anger, either. But I had no one to blame besides myself for all these maddening exercises.

"How do you feel?"

"Fracking exhausted. Also grouchy and hangry, like a shark."

"Good. Now you can take a break and hit those books over there." Thurston pointed at a bare table.

I knew the tablet resting on its top held several stacks of books on extrahuman history but it still looked heavy. Trudging over there felt like shuffling out of bed at zero dark thirty in the morning to change a dirty diaper. Had it already been almost six years? Would I ever even see my daughter's face again?

The thoughts knocked all my anger flat on its back, turning it turtle until I felt its flip-side, despair. I sat and ran one hand down my face. When I looked at the table again, a plate hovered near my elbow, then drifted left until it came to rest near my right hand. Four frosted donuts and a napkin sat before me, like an undiscovered shore. I stormed the plate.

Keeping the jelly from sticking to my lips and tusks was easy. I vanquished the donuts soundly, their remains fueling this next challenge to my concentration.

I hit the virtual books, figuratively. Each of the volumes Headmistress Thurston had compiled had a pretest at the beginning. About three hours later, I'd whipped some CLEP butt.

It was just Multiple Guess and True or Fake exercises, but the piddly little quizzes opened my eyes. I knew more than I thought I did. If the info in those questions reflected the CLEP's content, I'd be golden in extrahuman history. I stood up, resisting the urge to stretch or show any other sign that the chair had made my entire backside fall asleep.

"Is that all you got, Thurston?"

"Of course not." She raised an eyebrow. "If I'm not tough enough for you, I could send Professor Watkins here early instead."

"Um, no. Sorry."

I'd heard stories about Nate Watkins, that he'd endured a coma for almost six months. When asked how he held on, the Professor only said he needed to hand out more failing grades to first-year students under the impression they knew extrahuman anything. His reputation looked worse on paper than any other faculty member at the school, but the students who liked him defended his methods like fanatics.

"Don't be sorry, be studying." Henrietta Thurston produced her wand from nowhere and tapped my tablet with it.

The screen flared, then shut off and on again, as though it had widened one flat eye and then winked. The display now showed more material, again stuff that wasn't new.

"Extrahuman Faerie Ecology?" I snorted. "Don't make me laugh."

"Lynn Frampton finished the same intensive on this subject in two hours." The Headmistress smirked. "Think you can outdo a mundane Freshman?"

"Great Garters, yes!"

I raced through, barely needing to spend over five minutes per twenty-page unit for the Unseelie sections. The Seelie ones took longer. I knew more about Grims and Gnomes than Sprites, brownies, and Pixies. Imps were a total mystery, to the point where I missed almost all the pretest questions about them.

The imps were wizened little creatures, similar in looks to Gnomes except that they had their own teeth and didn't shave their beards. But that's where the similarities ended. Gnomes refracted time by a few minutes in either direction. Imps worked flat-out miracles but only for a price. Usually it was an item or immediate service of value but on rare occasions they'd ask a future favor.

I squinted at the electronic entry before me. The passage about those rarely asked-for favors was highlighted. I wondered who'd done that. The last thing I wanted to do was ask Thurston a stupid question.

Filing my suspicions away for later took willpower. Good thing I'd developed that in spades since my literal affair with impulsiveness resulted in becoming another teen pregnancy statistic.

I quit my internal whine-fest. I was here now, at college with a second chance. Life gave those, sometimes, even if the Faerie monarchs didn't. I'd been scoffing at Thurston's blistering lesson plan, thinking her school and the mortal world it catered to was soft and weak. I closed my eyes for a moment, the visual echo that the screen's glow left on the back of my eyelids lingering.

Maybe the world wasn't too soft. Or I'd grown too hard. The only luxury I'd allowed myself for seven years was love for my kid. I had to be soft with her because that's what kids need. But that love, gentle as it might be, still surged wilder than the stormiest sea.

The memory of that feeling stayed with me when I opened my eyes. One glance at the clock told me I'd never beat Frampton's record if I didn't buckle down. She might have made that time trying to prove herself competent in a school full of extrahumans. But I had the one person I loved more than anything else in either world at stake. When I set the tablet down, I gazed at the three-handed face on the wall.

I'd beaten Lynn Frampton by seven seconds.

"Piece of cake."

"Tomorrow Captain Tolland." Henrietta Thurston opened the door, letting air from the disused hallway into the classroom. "Bright and early, oh-five-hundred hours."

I shuffled out of the room, waving my hand once in farewell. Pausing, I gazed down the long hallway toward the door at the end where I could see the regularly paced students bustling by on their way to dinner.

"Aye aye, ma'am."

Headmistress Thurston had earned my respect. On that day, she had me convinced I could handle this challenge and study my way back into my daughter's immediate presence again.

Neither of us had any clue how wrong that idea was.

Hope

"Lady Harcourt, may we visit with the baby egg please?" I ducked my head in a sort of bow because I hate curtsies. Ed put his hand on his tummy and did a proper one. I bet his brother Sir Fredrick had taught him that.

"That's may. And yes." The dragon lady everyone and their Grandma was scared of smiled and opened the blanket so I could get a look.

"Thanks!" I put my hands together. Not to clap, just so I didn't make a mistake. See means look, not touch and no matter how nice the dragon lady seemed now, that'd change fast if we spooked her. "Hey, why's it got blue and green spots?"

"Those colors come from their parents," said Ed. "The spots tell us that baby's mom has Poison magic and the dad was an Air dragon."

"Was?" I blinked, then bit my tongue to keep from saying the horrible thing. The poor baby dragon wasn't even born yet and was half an orphan already. I remembered Mama talking to Grandpa about how a dragon named Wilfred got killed by Pharaoh's rats a bunch of months ago. I looked at my shoes instead of the egg. There's something you're supposed to say to someone when a person they care about dies, so I did.

"Sorry, Missus Harcourt."

"Thank you, child." Her eyes got all glittery, but she didn't cry. That made no sense, mostly because she wasn't a Pirate. But what if she was something like a Ninja or a Viking that didn't cry?

Or maybe dragons couldn't cry. She could have got used to not crying. I wasn't sure what to say next, but Ed figured it out. Of course. He seemed like a teacher's pet kind of kid besides being older than me.

"If you don't mind, I have a question about dragons, Mrs. Harcourt."

"I'll probably answer it, but you'll never know if you don't ask."

"Okay." Ed chewed on his bottom lip, the way Grandpa always did when he had to write a court letter to the king. "Two dragons always make an egg. But what about a dragon and someone who isn't one? After she marries Blaine, will Kim Ichiro lay eggs like you did?"

Hertha Harcourt's face got all scrunched, like when you bite a lemon. And then she leaned against the wall behind her and laughed. The egg in her arms bounced up and down the same way humans bounced their tiny babies. I saw a shimmer around it like a smile, even though eggs don't have faces. Well, not unless you draw one on with a marker.

"It's more that only two dragons ever produce eggs, Edward. And please, both of you, call me Hertha." Hertha dabbed the corners of her eyes. "No, Kim won't lay eggs. She'll have babies the usual way and if we're lucky, they'll grow into dragons. Girls, I hope."

"Yeah!" I pumped my fist in the air. "Girls are awesome!"

Ed's eyes moved to the left, right, and back again. He shrugged. Hertha shook her head.

"Yes, Hope, I agree that girls are awesome." She patted the egg that sat in her lap now. "But the reason I hope my grandchildren are girls is that there aren't too many dragons in the world anymore. The ones left who can still have babies are boys, except me."

I didn't bother saying that Hertha was a girl because I didn't want to be like Captain Obvious. His name was really Ozymandias but I always call him Obvious because that's how he talks. Everyone puts up with it because he rescued a bunch of extrahumans a hundred years ago or something. I realized that I'd probably never see Obvious or any of my other Unseelie friends again. I looked away from Hertha and her egg.

"Hope?" A hand not much bigger than mine patted my elbow. "You okay?"

"Dunno." I looked up. "Maybe I miss Mama a little."

"Yeah, me too. A little." Eyes like the sky peered out from under bangs that needed a bowl and a pair of scissors. After that, Ed looked past me.

I turned to see who he'd rolled his eyes at and came face to face with the ghost lady. She had two long black braids and wore a red flannel shirt with scuffed boots over dirty jeans. Something like belts crossed her shoulders, and I remembered the harness Grandpa wore his pistol in. Hers was more old-timey, though. Dustier too.

"Quit making googly eyes at us, Kasa." Ed shook his head. "Anyway, I need you to go check on some things for me."

"Don't you mean people, kid?" Her laugh reminded me of wild dogs. "And why should I do what you say?"

"You ghost, me medium, that's why." Ed crossed his arms. He

looked a little silly, standing up to an armed lady twice his height. Did I look like that? It didn't matter. Ed was right; she was a ghost, and he was a strong Psychic. He could order her if he wanted.

"Fine. I get it." Kasa smirked. "You catch a case of regrets and want me to check on your family. But I—"

"I know. You can only check on Fred because ghosts can't cross between the Under and the mortal realm."

"Is that ghost giving you trouble, Edward?" Hertha peered at the air around Kasa.

I could tell she couldn't see dead people like Ed and me could. Good thing, too. A dragon medium would be super powerful, which also means scary. If you don't believe me about power being scary, you haven't been paying attention. Start. Anyway, Kasa answered Hertha.

"Tell her I'm not." The ghost turned her back and waved, heading off through the wall to the courtyard. "See ya!"

Explaining the whole ghost business to a dragon lady distracted me from all the sad stuff for a while. And then, Ed pretended with me that the giant tree jungle gym thing was a real pirate ship. And after that, even though the sun stayed in the middle of the sky, we got sleepy because it was way past our bedtimes.

We fell asleep in hammock-like branches, listening to Hertha sing lullabies to her egg.

CHAPTER FOUR

Albert

"Your Majesty." I took a knee. The gesture felt more hollow than the old oak by the Planetarium in Roger Williams Park, but less rotten. I was the biggest stinker.

"Sir Albert, rise." The queen sat on her throne more than in it.

She never quite seemed to be in anything at all. I always thought that part of her lived elsewhere, the observation a luxury most of her subjects didn't have. One of the few who did sat at her left. Richard Hopewell didn't deserve a full glance. The view from my peripheral vision was too much and even added something extra to my observation.

Hopewell's glamour, the magic hiding his faerie side, had grown patchy and tattered. Even his ability to cast multiple schools of magic couldn't stop the inevitable need to choose a Monarch and tithe. His time was shorter than even Fred Redford's had grown the day he rescued his brother from this throne room.

Why hadn't the Redcap knight returned with Bianca Brighton from the beach? She'd fallen through a portal over it the night

27

before. I'd sent a message to Fred via Pixie, but heard nothing back.

"I take it the children are with their protector in the nursery." The queen hadn't asked a question. She wasn't born at night, let alone last night, or so rumor had it. Both Monarchs kept their origins a mystery. Maybe they hadn't been born at all in the usual sense.

"Yes, Majesty."

"Good. Then you can give me your version of the tale about why my suitor is unable to return to the mortal realm."

I explained without preamble or excuse, giving her information as she always compelled. Twice per week, the Sidhe Queen expected my figurative guts to spill in front of her and the evil suitor who used all my information against my classmates. The queen wanted nothing but facts, regardless of how many mistakes I made in the process of getting them. And she trusted Richard.

The truth-inducing arrow Olivia Adler had shot Gino Gitano with meant all of Richard's skeletons emerged from their closets. An unflinching narcissist, Gino would leverage his inability to lie for the rest of his life in his favor, as far as courts of law were concerned. The queen's court was another matter.

"I'm giving a standing order to detain Gino Gitano on sight and brought to my demesne." The queen's voice rang with magical authority though her eyes remained flat, the usual twinkle gone.

Any of her standing orders carried through the entirety of her half of the Under and this one was no exception. I set my features into a mask of dutiful neutrality and nodded, confident that my puzzlement wouldn't show. A lifetime of hiding my true feelings meant only a Telepath or Precog could know my heart without my consent.

I couldn't figure out why she hadn't given a kill order. If Richard Hopewell was important to her, either for love or power, detainment was a weak response to the threat Gino posed. I didn't dare question my Queen, however. Risking her wrath or indebtedness was a zero-sum game.

"Majesty." The voice came from the queen's right. I knew better than to assume that space was empty. A long, tall, slender creature stood there, easily mistaken for a stalk of bamboo. I knew better.

"Speak your piece, Brownie."

"Gitano is too dangerous to leave walking the mortal realm. In a legal sense, his presence there could cause trouble for Seelies in the mortal courts of Law."

"That is why I have a duchess and a knight working in the mortal courts. You know nothing."

The brownie stood, remaining silent, but it crackled, bending as though the queen's dismissal had been a strong gale. I understood how it felt only a moment later as she turned her attention my way again.

"Tell me about this errand you sent Sir Frederick on."

"A friend came through a portal unintentionally, Majesty. Due to the delicate nature of your new long-term guest, I sent my peer on the mission I could not manage alone."

"You shouldn't have and you will not in the future."

"As you wish, Majesty."

"Sir Frederick will answer to me with the results of said mission. You will concern yourself with it no longer."

I hid my blinking by pushing my hair behind one ear. In the mortal realm, I'd have pushed my glasses up my nose but I didn't need those here. Counting to three, I breathed in and then out the same way. Only after two repetitions did I realize that the queen's order stood unanswered.

"Understood, Majesty."

"Mere understanding is not enough, Sir Albert."

"Yes, your Majesty. However, I must advise, a promise of

obedience may not be the wisest course in the matter of a medium's presence in the Under."

"So, there is more to this errand of Sir Frederick's than its surface appearance." The queen closed her eyes. I measured the moments and found them longer than the day Fred had tithed to her in the thirteenth hour of his Quest to save his brother. "Richard, it's time."

The nemesis in yellow bowed and murmured something to her I couldn't make out. The queen blushed, bringing back a memory I hadn't revisited for close to a decade, since Prep School at Trout Academy. Back then, I'd evoked the same response in Gemma Tolland. A sour emotion dropped in the pit of my stomach, a grim and familiar sort of gravity.

"Sir Knight, you will announce to the court that the time is nigh." The queen's voice sang with the power of her full authority. "Richard Hopewell will tithe to my service at the thirteenth hour tomorrow. Assemble my guests. You are dismissed."

I had no choice but to do as she commanded.

Ed

The Sandman must have visited. I wasn't sure whether he was real or what kind of extrahuman he'd be if he was, but my eyes sure felt gritty when I rubbed them. After that, I waved the arm I wasn't lying on at whatever had broken into my snooze time.

"Go 'way, 'm sleepin'." Something like that came out of my mouth, anyway.

"No." Something cold poked my cheek. Kasa didn't understand that I lived with the most prankish poltergeist in Rhode Island, which made me immune to most ghostly tactics. "Wake up, kid. It's important."

"Ed." This new voice was familiar. My best grown-up friend besides Fred.

"Bianca?" I opened my eyes and wished I hadn't.

After that, I opened my mouth but sound and breath left before I could think of words to go along with them. My brother, my personal hero, had run off to rescue Bianca Brighton. Disbelief got in a fistfight with disappointment, short-circuiting my brain like a smartphone in a toilet. Thoughts swirled.

Bianca was the second youngest medium on Rhode Island's Registry and I was the first. She'd done a lot to help me, especially after my mom got arrested for putting Professor Watkins in a coma. If it hadn't been for Bianca, the ghosts at our house might have gone from helping to one of the worst hauntings in over a hundred years.

A kid medium like me couldn't handle that many ghosts. The rule was one for every year you'd been able to see them. Bianca helped by moving some, coaxing them over to the college or public works, or helping them move on. Instead of the thirty ghost crew, our house back on the East Side only had seven now.

The overworked girl hovering in the air next to my hammock had lived through a fatal-to-others car accident, the Nocturnal Lounge's destruction, and a pair of Mafia hitmen. It wasn't the slow-fall wards keeping her aloft, either. She'd died and, from the looks of her ghost, the diabetes had done her in.

"Oh no." Hope's warm hands gripped my arms, resting her pointy chin on my shoulder. Rainbow wings wrapped around me, stilling shivers I'd barely noticed "She's stuck here, without her ghost friend."

"Look, I have to talk fast. Quiet, too." Bianca glanced at Hertha. The dragon lady still slept, curled on a bench around her egg.

"Okay." I nodded.

"Hopewell didn't bother killing me. He just took my purse and tossed it into a portal he'd made. It's why I'd died. My insulin was in there. But anyway, I also had something else. A box."

Bianca scrunched her forehead and put her hands flat in front of her, turned up like she held a bowl.

The air just above her hands got darker, turning into some kind of rectangular box. Marks etched their way into its sides. Those marks reminded me of the decorations my dad put on the stuff he made.

"It's important." Hope whispered. "Not the box, what's in it."

"Yeah, you get it." Bianca smiled. "Good. So, you need to get the box to the right person."

"When's it supposed to do that?"

"I don't know. But Duke Ismail told me that a Sprite gave it to him. It's important." Bianca glanced at Hertha and then the door. "I gotta get out of here."

"Out of where?"

"The queen's demesne, and before Hopewell tithes. He technically killed me and if I'm not in the king's side of the Under before everything he's done goes to the Seelie crown, I'm stuck in this castle like Kasa here. Anyway, this is important. Just get the box back."

"He'll do it." Hope opened her wings instead of shouting, making the hair fly back from my face.

"Wait a minute, wouldn't it be better to get Al or—" I swallowed my brother's name. Bianca wouldn't want him on this box retrieval thing. She said she didn't blame him to make me feel better. I shrugged. "Someone who's not a kid?"

"Nope." Bianca shook her head, then glanced at Hertha again. Had the dragon lady moved? I didn't know. "You're perfect. Hopewell will underestimate you for sure. But he'll only make that mistake once, so you get one shot each. I'd wish you good Luck but I think you can do it without that."

A soft whimper came from the bench below. I peered down at the dragon and her egg. Hertha had definitely moved this time. When I looked up again, Bianca and Kasa had gone.

CHAPTER FIVE

Gemma

"This time, the gloves come off, Thurston!" My voice sailed out on a plume of mist, a sign that the evening's temperatures might dip below freezing. Cold or not, being outside felt like freedom after fourteen hours in the library with the CLEP tablet.

"Bring it!" The Headmistress smirked and tilted her eyes up at the Jack-o'-lantern hovering a few feet above her head.

I stretched my arms out, harnessing currents of wind off the water. It whipped away all the treble from the vampire Punk band practicing on the far side of India Point Park before rushing up and then down. The carved orange face mocked me by only bobbing slightly instead of ending up over the Headmistress's face.

"Come on, Tolland, is that all you got?"

"No!" I lied. It pretty much was, without a wand to focus the magical air energy I barely ever used. When you know for sure you'll grow up to be a Troll, you don't much bother with a side-power like air magic. It blows.

Before Henrietta Thurston could call me out for fibbing the

Jack-o'-lantern sailed gracefully down to rest on the ground behind her. She turned her head to watch three and a half suits stride across the lawn toward us. The fourth figure wore jeans and a mullet.

"Professor Thurston, we have some questions for you." A perky brunette smiled and flashed a badge. Federal.

"And you are?" Thurston's saucy expression had morphed into an icy calm.

"Natalie Johnson, FBE." She tilted her head at the tall guy next to her. "This is my partner, Agent Derek Dennison."

"It's good to see you again, Headmistress." Agent Dennison grinned. "And thanks for your part in getting me reoriented after my, um, stay in the Under."

"I'd appreciate an explanation instead of thanks, Agents." She crossed her arms.

"We were part of a RECO unit investigating the Gatto Gang but current circumstances here changed our orders." Agent Johnson shrugged with one shoulder, bouncing her hair.

"So what are you looking for from me, exactly?"

"There's an item of interest." Agent Dennison cleared his throat, tugging at the tie collaring him. If one of these Feds was the "bad cop" I couldn't tell which. "We need to search for it in every magically enhanced building at three locations in the state."

"Let me guess. One of these is my school." She sighed. "I assume you wouldn't be here if you hadn't already got warrants."

Dennison nodded. "And the other is the Harcourt mansion in Newport." He jerked his chin at the pair behind him. "That's why we have Weaver and Klein with us. They have a question for you."

"Where's Hertha Harcourt?" Detective Klein pulled no punches. He stood with his feet apart, hands on his hips pushing the puffy orange vest to either side. That and the mullet fluttering in the mid-autumn breeze gave his attempt at assertiveness a thick coating of corny with a side of ridiculous.

Henrietta Thurston sighed and shook her head. The Detective locked gazes with her, eyes narrowing. If he hadn't looked so much like Michael J. Fox in Back to the Future, I wouldn't have laughed. I put my hand over my mouth right after, a second too late. I'd attracted some of the most negative attention in the near vicinity.

"There's nothing funny about our case, Tolland." Detective Weaver stepped forward, one hand drifting to the cuffs at her waist. Iron ones. "Your presence here stinks to high heaven, though, especially with your record."

"She's with me, Weaver." The Headmistress tilted her head. "You're looking at the most recent recipient of the Thurston Family Scholarship."

"Oh really? Then teach her about how nobody laughs at my partner except me."

Agent Dennison mumbled something about how I wasn't so bad but nobody paid attention.

"Consider it done." Thurston nodded. "But as to your question about Hertha, I don't have an answer for you."

"Who do you have an answer for, then?" Klein tapped his foot. "I want to be there when they ask it."

"I'm not being dodgy, Detective. I truly don't know where Hertha's off to. But if you want to investigate at the Harcourt home, I can direct you toward her son, Blaine."

"Living on campus again, is he?"

"Yes. Hutchinson dorm, first floor. But he's probably at the dining hall having dinner at this hour."

Klein said nothing, just strode off across the park and toward the East Side of Providence.

"We'll head over there, then." Weaver paused. "Good luck with Tolland. She's a handful."

"The handfuls always make the best students."

My face heated. The Headmistress applied her sass to every-thing, even propping up the reputations of former problem children. Or maybe she had an old grudge match with Detective Weaver. She waited until after the detectives had walked away to speak again.

"What do you expect from a spider shifter?" Thurston shrugged. "Venom, prickliness, and a long spool of memory all wrapped up in a predatory package."

"True story." Agent Dennison smirked.

I placed his surname. This Federal agent was Josh Dennison's missing big brother. He'd vanished while the rest of us were either still in High School or waiting for it with expectations loftier than a dragon's attitude. I took a gamble.

"From one problem kid to another, thanks."

"Nah, don't mention it." Agent Dennison stuck out his hand. "You had a hand in getting me out of the Under."

"Just say you're welcome already and move on, okay?" Agent Johnson waved one hand in my general direction. "We've got a big campus to search."

"Can it wait until tomorrow?" Agent Dennison shuffled one foot against the grass. "We still have to get paper warrants from the Night court."

"Well, we thought it'd be less disruptive if we had a look at all the diurnal spaces tonight and the nocturnal ones tomorrow, if that makes sense?" Agent Johnson was way too bubbly to be a Fed. Maybe that was one reason they'd given her a badge.

"It does." Headmistress nodded. "But you're interrupting a directed studies practicum here."

"No worries, we can wait until you're finished." Agent Natalie Johnson smiled. "I can watch a good magic practical any day of the week. And Derek here loves Punk music." She beckoned to Agent Dennison, who followed her all the way over to the stage where Lane Meyer's band practiced.

"But this isn't the test." I didn't dare even glance at the Headmistress as I protested. For all I knew, she could have been grading me for real all day.

"Whatever it is, we shall get back to it Miss Tolland. This time, you will take up the wand you didn't use last night."

This time, I had no choice but to take my twenty paces and turn to face her. The Jack-o'-lantern lifted in the air above her head again. Pulling the wand from where I'd tucked it into my belt felt like a cop-out. No self-respecting faerie used magus props for glamour or any other fae magic. But my Air stuff came from my mortal side, something I tried to forget about. I'd looked down my nose at the girl I'd been in High School for seven years, punishing myself for trusting a Sidhe.

Maybe it wasn't about self-respect. Learning about all kinds of magic was the goal here, how it worked overall. More self-awareness might hurt in the short-term but almost everyone I admire has that. Instead of using my magic to shout down the wind, I pointed the wand at the carved gourd and tried to imagine myself directing it like a conductor with an orchestra.

The Jack-o'-lantern bobbed down immediately, but then back up again in the Headmistress's more experienced magical hands. I rolled my eyes and focused on something over Thurston's shoulder so I could take a handful of deep breaths and refocus my energy.

The punk band played up on the small stage provided by Providence Parks and Recreation. Lane stepped back, letting his guitarist have the stage for a solo. Without magical interference, the wind carried a riff so sick it'd go as viral as swine flu if only someone recorded them. I dropped my wand arm, impressed.

Agent Natalie Johnson held her phone up, doing just that. Her partner, Derek Dennison, stood there staring at the performance like it was a glass of water and he hadn't had a drop to drink for three days. No, not the performance. Matt, the Night Creatures guitarist. I filed the information away for a future conversation with Josh. Better for him to learn that his werewolf brother had a crush on a vampire some place quiet. Romance between opposing factions only ended in disaster. I was living proof of that.

Pointing the wand again, I stared daggers at the jeering face on the Headmistress's pumpkin. I hadn't meant to unpack all the old Albert Dunstable-induced hand-staple-forehead moments, but they popped out like Jacks-in-the-box. I snorted.

"Jack trumps Jack." I punctuated that sentence with a focused jet of wind from the tip of the wand, steady and strong. Angst flowed out with it, teenage and otherwise.

The dumb pumpkin resisted as the Headmistress pushed back with her own air magic. Nevertheless, I persisted, but without the results I'd originally expected. Instead of crashing down on Thurston's head, the Jack-o'-lantern squashed, caving in on itself inches from her hair.

I called back my magic, letting the air go its own way. The lump of pumpkin puree floated into a trash can before the Headmistress dropped her own spell. She nodded at me, then put her wand away. I followed her lead and also her footsteps as she headed across the park toward the agents in charge of investigating her school.

Henrietta Thurston kept a near-perfect illusion of calm. Mostly, she seemed iced-over, safe behind a layer of something that made her untouchable. The one time I'd seen that layer crack was the night she took up the Kitsune tails, reviving an extinct magical shifter type.

Impossible was the word I would have used to describe my current situation. Identifying with the Headmistress of PPC was an idea I'd have laughed at only a few days earlier. But we had more in common than not. The biggest difference was that she navigated her course with more grace in her figurative pinkie than I had in my whole literal body.

She'd all but vowed to get revenge on her ex-husband the Extramagus. I wondered how she'd manage that under all the emotional armor and law enforcement scrutiny. It seemed as unlikely as getting my daughter back, but somehow, Headmistress Thurston seemed like a woman who could do five impossible things before breakfast. I had no way to even guess the outcome of her voyage.

Was Henrietta Thurston my Janey-come-lately role model? The only thing I could do was follow her and find out.

Hope

Grandpa always said to never wake a sleeping dragon, but I wasn't sure I could keep quiet. That's why I jumped out of the tree at an angle and let the slow fall wards set me down a few steps from the door. But before I could reach out to open it, Ed stepped in front of me.

He didn't say a word, just shook his head. When I rolled my eyes, he put his hands on his hips. I tried ducking around him but my wings got in the way. Finally, I won by taking a deep breath and acting like I'd scream.

After opening the door, I headed into the hall where it was bright as day even though my brain told me it was night time. Ed followed, probably trying to keep me out of trouble or whatever. At least he made sure the door shut behind me all nice and quiet.

"You suck at playing chicken, Ed."

"Maybe that's because I don't have wings." He trotted to catch up even though we were about the same size. "It's not a good idea, being out at this hour. It looks like daytime, but it's not. And there are scary things with more power at what passes for the night here."

"What would you know?" I snorted. Sometimes, Ed acted like he was seventy instead of seven. Nothing in Seelie could be as scary as Grims or other woojie stuff in the king's side of the Under.

"For your information, I've had four whole months of sleepovers in this castle." Ed stuck out his lower lip and tried to blow his bangs out of his eyes. They fell right back down again. "I know plenty. Anyway, there's no point to going now."

"Why?" It felt cool, being able to ask another person questions. I was used to everything and everyone in Faerie owning me if I asked too many. Ed was only a psychic though. I could ask him anything at all. Having a psychic friend could be cool if only he'd stop acting like the world's biggest know it all.

"It's all stuff for the bigs at this hour." He tried grabbing my hand.

"You sound like a big, with your at this hour stuff." I moved it out of the way.

"Well you sound like a baby, just wanting something for the sake of having it."

"I don't want to go out here for no reason. The ghost ladies gave us a quest and I take those seriously, mister."

"Mister? Jeez." He rolled his eyes. "This isn't a good time to call me an old fogie."

"Carp a something or other." I snapped my fingers. "Not the fish, that's carp. I mean like grabbing a moment or whatever."

"*Carpe diem*? There's never a real *noctem* here."

"Whatever." I didn't get his joke but didn't want to sound dumb. "Anyway, I'm gonna find that box."

"No way. I'm gonna."

I laughed. Ed had no experience going on quests. I did. Then again, maybe he didn't know that.

"Look, I know what I'm doing here. Grew up helping my family out with quests. So, don't slow me down, okay?"

"We're not supposed to look together, remember?"

"Oh." I peeked at him from out of the corner of my eye. He'd just asked me a second question and already owed me one. If he got into my debt three times without paying some back, he'd owe me his life. I kept my mouth shut because I wasn't sure whether I wanted it or even knew what to do with a medium's life, anyway. "So go back to bed, Ed."

"You."

"No. I got here first."

"Kids, hmm." The voice came from an open doorway to our left. It sounded creakier than fifty rusty hinges moving at the same time. "I haven't seen children here in an age."

"Um, thanks, I guess." I stepped forward, trying to peek into the room the voice came from.

"Do not go in there." Ed's hand grabbed mine, holding on tight. It was clammy, too. Ick.

"It's okay, young man." The voice replied. "You're right to be concerned and correct. Neither of you should enter my rooms if you value your lives."

I stopped with one foot in the air. I wouldn't take a triple dog dare to go in there now. Something in the squeaky old voice gave me creeps the size of Texas. I stepped back, next to Ed.

"I bet you can't come out of there."

"Oh, I certainly can. It merely takes an old soul like me a very long time to do so." I heard a few clicks and then a rustle, like fabric and the snap on an old pair of jeans.

"You wouldn't come out now."

"I would," the voice said. "As a matter of fact, I'm in the process of doing exactly that. Perhaps you'll wait for an old creature."

"Perhaps not." Ed stepped back, dragging me by the hand.

"Why, Ed?" I tried to follow him but my feet didn't want to move. When they finally did, it was hard to get them unstuck from the floor. It was like being inside a movie theater that hadn't been cleaned or something.

"That's a *Tsuchigomo* in there."

"Bless you."

"I didn't sneeze."

"Okay, so what did you say? In English, okay?"

"Spider goblin."

"Not a spider shifter?"

"No." Ed's hand had gotten even sweatier. "He's something completely different, not even a faerie. Spider shifters are related to these guys, but only like a puppy dog is to wolves."

"So you're telling me the guy in there couldn't turn into a spider, he actually is a half-and-half one. Like a mermaid?"

"Yeah, okay. Something like a mermaid. That makes sense since they're not faeries either." Ed kept dragging me down the hall toward the nursery. "Except instead of being half-fish and half-person, *Tsuchigomo* are half-spider and half-person. Kids disappear when they're around him, too."

Ed didn't have to say anything else, or drag me anymore either. Instead, I ran ahead so fast he had a hard time keeping up. We didn't stop until we got to the door to the treehouse room.

"So, will you go back in there already?"

"Yeah, sure, fine. Whatever." I stood with my hands at my sides, not reaching for the doorknob yet. "So I'll look for that box tomorrow."

"Good plan." Ed managed a shaky grin. "But we're not out of the woods. We still gotta sneak past the dragon lady."

We managed that just fine. Getting back to sleep was easy, too. Being out of danger was like Halloween night an hour after candy.

The next morning, not so much.

CHAPTER SIX

Albert

I rubbed the bridge of my nose, pushing my glasses up as I tried to get rid of the headache that had my sinuses in a death grip. The trip back to the mortal realm had been easy but staying awake while sitting in the night court after twenty hours wasn't. The jury foreman's voice amounted to white noise in my poor ears, even though he announced something we'd all been waiting months for.

"On all three charges of Crimes Against Extrahumanity, we find the defendant, not guilty."

Relieved sighs and angry rustles danced an echo in the yawning stone chamber. Karen Gunn, the prosecutor, slammed something against her table. I winced and pushed my glasses up again to rub the bridge of my nose.

"You okay, man?" I turned to find the contingent from Tinfoil Hat seated in the row behind me. Tony had spoken.

"Just need some Excedrin or something."

"Here." Olivia shoved her open handbag at me.

"Thanks." I plucked the lone green and white bottle from

among pens, books, and orange prescription bottles of stronger stuff. "You could run a pharmacy out of that bag."

"Meh." She shrugged. "I only kept it for being diurnal when I visit home. My parents are on the older side, so they like their early-bird specials."

"Ha!" Kim Ichiro's barking laugh had me wincing again. "Sorry, Al." The tablet in her lap beeped.

"I'm not the laugh police." I dry-swallowed three of the white tablets. "Just a Sidhe with an aching head." Faeries weren't supposed to get monster headaches or need glasses, either, not even in the mortal realm, but I did anyway. Bad habits die hard.

"Still. I laughed right up in your ear." Kim shook her head. "And I'm trying to make more apologies than Lynn Frampton this month. LORA's already recorded nine for me and ten for her, so I'm about to catch up."

"It's nice to have goals." One Excedrin stuck on the way down, making my voice raspier than a Goblin's. I tried to clear it a few times and started hacking up a lung instead. This happened just as the room went silent, of course.

"Woah there." Tony slapped my back a few times, which did absolutely nothing to help.

"Hmm." Kim narrowed her eyes, then elbowed Tony out of the way and poked my left shoulder.

The sense of unease I'd been lugging around with me since Fred Redford tithed Seelie lifted. It was almost like getting off a plane, how the cabin depressurizes and your ears and balance feel almost normal again. The Tanuki must have turned my luck. The pill went down finally and I stopped coughing but too late to avoid attracting an entire courtroom of attention.

"If you're quite finished, Mr. Dunstable." Judge Fiori had me in the cross-hairs of her most withering side-eye.

"Yes, Ma'am." I served the respectful address with a side of nodding because that's what the occasion called for. I should have mentioned that no one can expect a person choking on analgesic tablets to keep from coughing. Would I ever just stick up for myself and say the right thing and not the polite one? The room got pin-drop quiet.

"Court is adjourned." The judge tapped her gavel, and the silence reversed.

The room bloomed with sound and the needle on my headache inched over into the red. Migraine territory. Fun. Leaning against the table, I managed standing, even if just to shuffle out from behind the table while making my movements look intentional. Two decades of practice does that to a person. After that, I straightened and paced away from the front of the courtroom with measured steps.

Navigating the crowd was the easiest part. Most folks at night court were nocturnal or even Unseelie and wanted to avoid contact with me. Unseelies faced execution and the non-faerie nocturnal set feared anything that looked like it could bring on the sunshine. Even though I didn't have Spectral magic at my disposal like my mother, I still looked the part. I thought that, if only I could make it out into the hall, I'd be okay.

I thought wrong.

Outside the courtroom, echoes increased exponentially and the flashes from mundane and magical cameras alike chewed holes in my field of vision like gypsy moth caterpillars with oak leaves. If it had been one or the other, I might have made it. But light and sound launched a concerted attack against my senses and overpowered me. It was all I could do just to keep on breathing without giving voice to my pain by shrieking in agony.

By three steps, I tasted blood. By six, I saw red to go with it and had to close my eyes to keep the light out. The entire world coated my senses with a caustic slime that burned through my body as it besieged my mind, warring with sanity. A rush of air cooled my burning cheeks, and the sound damped down to tolerable levels, a phenomenon that hadn't occurred in seven years.

"Gemma?"

"You're a wreck again, Al." Her voice came low and soft, carrying through the air barrier she'd made around me.

"I've been walking wounded for a long time." I wasn't talking about the migraines. She knew it, too.

"Not my fault or my problem." The tap of leather-soled boots approached at my right.

"You could just undo the hushing spell, leave me to suffer." I rubbed my temples, both ready for this conversation and dreading it at the same time.

"I'm angry, not cruel. That's your game."

"Fate is cruel." I opened my eyes but kept them on the floor, not daring to meet her gaze.

"Don't you dare put the blame on anyone but yourself. You promised to meet me, go together to tithe to His Majesty. You didn't show. If you had, things would be completely different and you know it."

And she was right. I could have kept on arguing, make excuses about being unable to fight my parents but those had been hollower than my heart all these years. Living a lie caught up with me the night Hope picked up that feather. No, before that, when I heard Gemma fished Lane Meyer and his friends out of the Bay. The queen's orders since then only magnified my level of deceit.

I'd abandoned the woman I'd promised to marry, build a family and future with. The worst part was that I went right on loving her. Seeing her again drove home the point in a much more primal way than most Seelie Sidhe were comfortable with. I still desired her. She deserved an honest answer, not the canned generalities Sidhe families raised their kids to use, and the queen reinforced.

"Yes, our lives would have been different but we can't live the might-have-beens. All we have is now and how things could be." I opened my eyes, finally risked meeting hers. They shimmered in the pop and the flash of media and amateur cameras alike, the hazel awash with more amber than green. Gemma's gaze stole my breath, as ever. I wondered for a moment whether our mingled regrets had given her the ability to turn me to stone where I stood.

"Al, I don't know what to say."

"I do. Thanks for remembering how I look while hiding a migraine. You rescued me tonight even though you had every reason to walk on by. You're my hero, Gemma Tolland."

"Unseelie troll captains can't be heroes for Seelie Sidhe knights."

"I know it's forbidden, but that's how I feel. Again, I thank you."

"Whatever. Don't mention it or something." She waved a hand.

"There is no whatever and I will mention it. You have my gratitude, Captain."

The mention of her title along with the third insistence on thanks twined together between us like a rope across a chasm. A Tanuki had turned my luck earlier. Perhaps that's why I took a step toward her instead of leaving the tenuous connection at that. My heart pounded in my chest and at my temples when I realized she hadn't taken a step back to compensate.

"You're welcome, I guess." She shrugged with one shoulder, the way she always used to. The motion tugged at some long-dormant thread connected to the very core of my being. Perhaps that's why I made that third bold move.

"Go out with me again."

"Go out? This isn't Trout Prep, and we're not untithed changelings anymore. We can't even hold hands. You're crazy, Al."

"Maybe. I still want to see you, sane or not." I held her gaze. The queen couldn't execute me for that.

"We're on opposite sides in the coldest war ever waged." She shuffled one of her feet.

"I don't care about that. I only ever cared about you, Gemma. And now there's Hope. Please, one date."

"You sound like a quirky '90s movie protagonist, chasing some Manic Pixie Dream Girl."

"Your favorite." The trace of a smile tugged at my mouth. I showed it mercy, let it live a little longer.

"Yeah, I'm a sucker for Natalie Portman in *Garden State*. So yeah, okay. I'll go. One date and that's it, but just so I can tell you all about Hope." She put her hands on her hips. "Now get out of here before Headmistress Thurston comes back with the FBE Agents and that warrant. I'm following them when they leave to investigate."

"Wait, FBE Agents?"

"Watch it Al, or you'll be in my debt."

"You didn't answer." She had to, another part of faerie law.

"Yeah, okay. Here's the story." She told me about how the Feds were getting ready to search the Providence Paranormal campus, how Newport PD had Blaine Harcourt in for questioning.

"I'd better talk to these agents. There's a development they need to know about."

And that's how I ended up giving a formal statement to the mortal authorities about my Faerie monarch, my first step toward coming clean. At least I could say that I did it for love.

Ed

I woke up to the sound of something crackling like a huge fire. Pushing away from the big treehouse in the nursery was my first instinct, and I did that right away. But it wasn't on fire like I'd feared. I looked around as I drifted through the air, trying to find what woke me up. But I saw nothing out of place.

Hope peeped at me from her hammock above, wrinkling her nose. That meant I hadn't imagined the burning-leaves smell. I remembered something Dad always told me when he talked about fire safety and headed to the hall door. It didn't feel hot when I pressed my hand against it, so I tried the one that led to the bathroom. Nothing there, either.

After catching Hope's eye again, I shrugged. She shook her head, then pointed at the window. Lifting my feet so my sneakers wouldn't squeak like mice from dragging on the floor, I had a look outside and found the source of the fire.

The tithing tree in the courtyard blazed with autumn color in place of all the dark green high summer leaves it'd worn just the day before. I'd never seen it like that, not in any of the twenty-four weekends I'd spent visiting Fred.

"What is it, Ed?" Hope tugged my sleeve, then didn't let it go. Her voice sounded so tiny compared to how it had been earlier.

"I only sort of know." My arm twitched because I wanted to shrug it but if I did that then my shirt would pull right out of Hope's hand. The last thing I wanted was to make a girl, littler than me, more scared than she already was. "It has something to do with tithing but I've never seen this when people pledge fealty to the queen before."

"The state of faerie education is appalling these days, honestly." Hertha Harcourt yawned behind us. "That the son of a Redcap and the daughter of a Troll wouldn't know how the queen's Tithing Tree works is a dreadful thing to contemplate."

"It'd be nice if a wise dragon lady helped us learn something, then." I glanced over my shoulder at Hertha. The corners of her mouth pointed at the floor and she shook her head.

"Well, you have your egg. Maybe your baby would like to hear a story about the tree and a little boy and girl can learn something at the same time." Hope held her hand close to her mouth, the fingers curled into a loose fist and her thumb pointing at her lower lip. I knew a valiant effort to keep from sucking your thumb when I saw it.

"I'd prefer singing to my egg-bound child, but you're the

Alkonost now, child. You need to know this sooner rather than later."

"Okay." Hope gave the dragon lady a nod that could have come straight out of a Shonen Anime.

This time I did shrug. If Hope Tolland was channeling Wendy Marvell or Alphonse Elric, she didn't need to treat my sleeve like a lifeline. I wanted it back already, like so many other things in my life.

Hertha didn't sound even a bit reluctant, spinning us a yarn about her old Goblin butler. Not old because of his age, but because she'd fired him after her husband got killed. Apparently, the butler had given the queen access codes to the Harcourt mansion while Richard was there. The dragon lady watched him tithe to the Sidhe Queen. The tree's leaves turned and then went up in flames the moment he pledged to follow and protect her laws, becoming a Lord in her court on his first day there.

"But why didn't that happen when my brother took his seat at her round table as a knight?"

"Because, while Frederick might have skipped the ranks of page and squire, he didn't come in with a noble's title. You must start as a Lord or higher for that. And the tree's brighter the higher said rank will be. The Tithing Tree burns with the queen's intention. From the looks of things, Her Majesty will start Richard Hopewell as a duke."

I fidgeted, not daring to open my mouth and let out all my thoughts. According to my brother, I had a talent for seeming calm even when most kids would freak out. I couldn't look at Hertha though. It was like an elephant in the room stood between me and her, one she couldn't or wouldn't see. I wasn't about to draw her attention to it either. But Hope walked right up to it and slapped it in the face.

"Mrs. Harcourt, why are you talking about these guys like they're heroes or something? I mean, the Goblin Lord and Mr. Hopewell got your husband killed."

Hertha's eyes glittered. Her skin did, too. Even with a magipsychic amulet suppressing her dragon form, she'd started scaling over.

"Um, Hope?" I stepped in front of her, not sure what good that would do. "You just pissed off a dragon. Don't forget that we're crunchy and good with ketchup."

"I don't care because it's just not right that those guys basically got away with putting Pharaoh's Rats in a dragon's house." She peeked over my shoulder, resting her chin on it. I felt a gust behind me as she opened her wings, too. "Anyway, she won't hurt us. Mrs. Harcourt's a mom. Moms do the right thing for kids, always."

"No." I tried shrugging her off but her grip was too tight. "Giving birth doesn't make a good mom. I'm living proof of that. My mother got herself sent to jail because she couldn't go without a ghostly partner."

"The young medium is right, Alkonost." Hertha's grin glittered with too-sharp teeth. "Some bonds and promises trump even motherhood. And besides, neither of you are my own children. The fact that I have a son and this egg gives you no immunity to my wrath. This is your final warning to stop provoking it. Storytime is over."

The dragon lady turned her back on us, crooning over the baby encased in its mottled shell. Heaven help us.

CHAPTER SEVEN

Gemma

I stomped out of the courthouse even though Albert Dunstable wouldn't hear anything loud for fifteen more minutes. I knew he followed along behind me, too. If Headmistress Thurston hadn't also been there, I might have turned around and called the whole ridiculous attempt at a date off.

Out in the chilly October air, my head cleared, which kicked it into high over-thinking gear. Why had I agreed to see him again? That pretty face, of course. The sight of him had my blood racing all over again. He'd barely changed at all and the little differences made him no less interesting. New wire-framed glasses replaced his old horn-rimmed clunkers which only made the dreamboat eyes more noticeable.

But I couldn't let myself get swept away again. Seelie and Unseelie faeries couldn't touch each other. Our so-called date had to stay platonic, or we'd both get executed. At least this meant he wasn't just looking for sex. Again.

Back in High School, Al was rational, a cool and steady hand at the wheel in a sea of a turbulent adolescence. Troll changelings had it the hardest, even worse than the Redcaps. Our faerie magic ran our tempers hot and most of us made choices that got us into trouble with Detective Weaver and her colleagues. Hertha Harcourt called them on me plenty of times, too.

I might have ended up in Juvie if it hadn't been for Al's calming influence. Dependable Dunstable, I used to call him, even though I didn't understand how he managed to be. He'd steered me out of worse trouble than he ultimately got me into. But when it came time for us to run off and tithe to the Goblin King, he stood me up. Forgetting that was impossible. Was I ready to forgive?

If it hadn't been for Hope, maybe I wouldn't be. And she was the real reason I'd agreed to the date, anyway. Civil relations with my baby's daddy couldn't hurt now that he had faerie-dictated custody. The fact that he'd been the man of my dreams since I'd been having them was only a fringe benefit.

I closed my eyes, nearly stumbling over a cobblestone as I walked up the hill and toward the college. Campus was a series of old brownstones lined up along two city blocks that only existed on maps made after the big Reveal. The whole thing was built by magi of various types and hidden by alumni who'd tithed to a Monarch after graduation. At all six corners sat larger brick buildings used as dorms, five stories each and square.

A quad ran along behind the brownstones, meaning nobody could park on campus, not even emergency vehicles. That's why the magic labs moved to a new space near the Observatory. The State of Rhode Island and Providence Plantations had safety regulations that the outed magical community had to follow. I had to cross the street to get to campus proper, so I followed the Headmistress to a corner, complete with crosswalk, and waited for the light to turn green.

Mortal laws were a cakewalk compared to the queen's. That was why most Seelie families managed them well enough to make up the vast majority of extrahuman lawyers. I stepped into the street. Yoshi Ichiro was unique as a shifter in legal practice. Law enforcement and extrahuman medicine were another story and part of the reason PPC ended up opening admissions to anyone with the grades.

I stopped walking. The open admissions had to be part of why Richard Hopewell turned against the school. He used to be a Professor here, used to be to Henrietta Thurston's husband, too, until the year before said change took effect.

"Hey, get out of the road, you dumb broad!"

A strident blast on a horn came with a free bird. I returned the favor by shooting one back at the angry driver. My light was still green but this piece of work wanted to turn right on red. That shifted my Troll temper up a notch higher than usual.

"This dumb broad can total your car with one punch, asshole!" I brandished a fist and dropped my Glamour to give him a good view of my tusks.

Rising windows squeaked and the soft thunk of locks engaged in an unsatisfying counterpoint. I itched for a fight I shouldn't get into but at that moment didn't care. The seven-year fire in my belly kicked up higher than ever. Trolls are built to destroy. Rage threatened to touch down like a tornado, savage in its hunger for destruction. At least I wouldn't be on campus when it swept in. Two steps separated me from the sidewalk at the boundary.

A familiar wave of power crashed around me, starving that rage, except it felt more like a force of will than any nameable school of elemental magic. I knew from experience that Air, Fire, Water, Umbral and Spectral each had a distinct identity. This had none. All the same, it felt warm, how room temperature seems after an hour out in freezing temperatures.

Logical people think two spells always pile up and do more damage, like a set of natural disasters. Magic isn't logic. If it were, the Monarchs wouldn't need rules. Magic also isn't a force of nature. It comes from inside us, it's part of us, something only we have the power to control—or not. And, whether between allies or enemies, it has a way of balancing out.

I'd almost let the asshole driver turn into the last straw on my back even though I didn't have to. But I didn't have to let that other magic, whatever it was, help me back down. I made the choice: static calm over raging destruction.

My fist stayed brandished as I stepped off the street and on to PPC property. The magic stayed behind me the whole time, like a good tailwind. The caster literally had my back.

"Broad as a term to describe a lady is crass in any case." Al's voice, of course. "Take care with your manners in the future."

Al came out from behind me, his own Glamour dropped as he stood at my side. We watched the driver lay down skid marks on the asphalt, his car squealing away. I probably shouldn't have looked at the Sidhe but since I'd behaved myself with the bad driver I indulged. I turned, tilting my head to look him full in the face.

Beautiful wasn't a word people used to describe most men. Albert Dunstable was not most men, even with the glamour that made faeries seem more human. Flowing platinum hair framed a face with fine-boned, symmetrical features. The glasses perched on the bridge of his nose only magnified the effect. Sidhe looked breakable, like creations of spun glass meant for decor, but their faerie magic made them sturdier than they appeared.

I glanced down at my un-Glamoured hands, gnarled and callused from years at sea in both the Under and the mortal realm. My nails, tough as steel, ended in points like any other Troll's. We're more powerful than we appear, too, but the only time we took anyone's breath away was when we knocked them out on the battlefield.

"Hey, Odd Couple," shouted a voice. "Catch up and make it snappy!"

The shouter was none other than Josh Dennison, leader of the pack everyone belonged to except me. He had a Klingon on his starboard bow, a tiny woman with stripy brown hair. I remembered Kim Ichiro from the Lane Meyer search and rescue adventure. Striding over, I peered at Josh

"Don't call us a couple."

The Tanuki chick raised an eyebrow, then scrunched them together as her eyes moved from me to Al and then back again like we played ping pong instead of just standing there like relatively normal people.

"Odd."

"Yeah, your Alpha already called us that." I shrugged. "Whatever. Anyway, Newport PD is interrogating your boyfriend, Ichiro. I should probably catch up with the Headmistress, so see you later."

As I power-walked toward Henrietta Thurston's retreating back, I heard Kim mention something about Al's luck and then my name. But I couldn't be bothered with Tanuki rumors while the Feds were on campus. I rolled my eyes at no one.

The Federal investigation came straight out of circumstances built by the guy trying to get the school shut down. If they found anything hinky, Richard Hopewell might just get what he'd wanted all along. But I couldn't let that happen. PPC was probably my only shot at seeing Hope again.

Hope

"Come on, Ed." I let go of his shirt with one hand and grabbed his arm with the other. "Step away from the angry dragon."

"Um." He looked at his shoes, so I did, too. They weren't untied or anything, so I pulled him along, heading for the door. He stumbled for one step but came along after.

The door wasn't easy to open with one hand, and Ed didn't help. I put my back into it like Mama always told me to do when

I helped swab the deck. My wings flapped out, and after that, the door moved like a scared rat.

I took a left this time, away from the creepy spider-goblin's room. I thought it was morning but didn't want to take any chances. The door clicked shut on its own. Ed planted his feet.

"What gives?"

"We have to go back and visit the *Tsuchigomo*."

"Oh, no. No way, Ed. I'm not going in there with an actual unfriendly spider-man. Unless he's a Peter Parker kind of guy, which I already know he isn't."

"It's daytime, though. He can't do a thing to us now."

"He wants to eat us." I wasn't about to tell Ed that spiders scared me more than anything in either world.

"He also said he had something to tell us."

"That's what I'd say if I wanted to eat someone and was too old and creaky to chase them."

"But it's the daytime—Look, I don't get it with you. You're not scared of sharing a room with a literal dragon lady who could poison us in our sleep, but you won't visit a little old spider-man who has no powers at the moment."

I blinked and dropped his arm. He was right, of course. The know-it-all.

"Hertha's supposed to watch us, though. The queen said so."

"Yeah, but that doesn't mean she's any safer than the *Tsuchigomo* in the daytime. Anyway, you can come with me or not. I'll have a chat with him."

I watched Ed's back getting smaller as he walked down the hall but couldn't let him go it alone. Psychics were almost human, especially a medium with no ghosts around. And yeah, I was only just human two days before. That's a lot of time for a kid. The Alkonost thing comes with this idea about what to do and what not to do. I can't explain it, but the rest of this adventure might.

Going after him was easy. He was taller, but I was still faster than Ed Redford, famous kid medium. Magic bird stuff kind of rocks. Okay, it's almost totally awesome, except for the whole automatically being Seelie part. Saying I didn't like the queen back then was a big fat lie. But I liked the creepy spider goblin even less.

Ed walked right up and knocked on the door to his room, which was closed now. I saw a mark on it, something that looked smeared on with finger paint sparkly enough to come from a unicorn. Except everyone said those don't exist.

"Come in."

That creaky old voice made all my feathers stand up. The hair on the back of Ed's neck did the same trick, but he twisted the knob and pushed the door open anyway. My face scrunched up because the nursery door opened in. I turned my head twice, like crossing the street. The spider goblin's door was the only one hung to keep something in instead of out. The queen wasn't stupid, then. Or at least only stupid about her jerk of a suitor. Maybe she was stupid about Hopewell the same way I was stupid about my dad, wanting to make him happy because she cared too much.

"Love stinks," I mumbled.

"What's that?" Ed looked over his shoulder with one foot on either side of the doorway.

"Nothing." I waved my hands at him, like shooing a fly. "Go, already."

He entered, and so did I.

The walls in there had white tapestries everywhere. I wrinkled my nose because that wasn't right somehow, but before I could put my finger on it, I saw the old fellow. He sat on a cushion like the Caterpillar in Wonderland with all eight of his legs folded under him.

"Shouldn't you be smoking?" I slapped a hand over my mouth. Hanging out with Ed and Hertha had made me forget that asking questions was a bad idea.

"Don't be ridiculous, child." The spider-goblin man-thing

tilted his head, making his neck crack. "My webs are too flammable for that."

"I'm Edward Redford, and I'm here because last night you said there's something we should know."

My mouth dropped open. Ed wasn't wasting any time here. He also looked directly at the creepy half-human creature, as though he was trying to ignore something else in the room I hadn't noticed yet. That only made me want to find whatever it was.

"Yes. You children seek a box."

"Well, duh. We're kids, and toy boxes are a thing." Maybe I shouldn't have sassed the old guy, but I didn't like how he knew about a quest we'd only just gotten.

"Hope, quit it."

"What? he's an unfriendly neighborhood spider-guy. I'm not going to treat him like we're bosom buddies."

"Still, he's offering us information, info we need. Tone back the sass already."

"Okay fine." I crossed my arms over my chest and folded my wings. Ed had a point, even if I didn't like it. I turned my nose up, then looked at the spider-man from the corner of my eye. This let me watch the curtain covered doorway at the back of the room, which Ed hadn't glanced at yet.

"So, you have something to tell us about a box." Ed's foot twitched, and I could tell he wanted to tap it but didn't dare.

"Yes. It's not here, but it needs to be. Unfortunately for you, your brother's friends made a mistake. They left it with someone they shouldn't have." The big bad spider-goblin clicked his feet. Not all of them, just maybe three. He had a few more working in his web, which he kept glancing at.

I wondered whether he saw and heard things through them. Spider shifters use their silk to hear and see things when they're not in the room. This guy was doing something like that, probably. I couldn't be sure. If I was a dragon or a magus, I might have been able to tell just by looking. But being the Alkonost meant that all I could see were annoying ghosts.

"So you said your information would help us. This isn't helpful."

"I said no such thing, but I know more than what I'm saying to you now. However, if you want to know it too, you must ask me directly."

"Oh. Being in your debt is dangerous." Ed folded his hands so tight, his knuckles whitened. "There has to be another way to do this."

"With all danger, what's most important is to decide which risks are worthy." Spider feet tapped again for a few moments. "It's up to you to decide whether you think this reward merits the debt."

"Nothing makes up for that." I tugged at my friend's sleeve. "Ed, we should get out of here."

I couldn't say anything about it in front of evil spider-man, but I'd seen something behind that curtain. Something that moved with hitches and jerks. There was no way for me to know what it was, but I didn't want to stick around and find out. Or worse stick around and end up back there with whatever it was.

"It's worth the risk. I'll do it." Questions spilled out of Ed's mouth on purpose, like the one time I'd seen Grandpa pour beer on a grave, instead of by accident like when I knock over my juice cup. "Where is the box? How do we get it? Where do we have to bring it?"

My mouth dropped open. With those three questions, Ed had put himself in debt to the spider-goblin. He was already in debt to me. I could use that somehow to cancel the favor out if it went bad. I tried not to watch the thing behind the curtain while I waited for the answers to Ed's questions.

"The box is in the mortal realm but hidden from most. You get it by finding Joyce Watkins, and you bring it back here to the Under."

Ed held up one finger and opened his mouth. I understood what that meant; he wanted to ask another question. I shook my head. Those answers could only be meant to get my buddy to ask even more questions and make an even bigger debt. But my warning worked. Being smart makes a big difference to a measly medium in a faerie court.

"Thank you for the answers, Sir." Ed bowed his head. "I will use them as best I can."

"Yeah, now it's time to go. We have curfews and stuff like that. I mean, we're kids, you know?"

"Oh, yes, I am well aware." More legs clacked, majorly giving me the creeps. I'm usually pretty brave, but spiders scare me. The only thing that could have spooked me more was the giant squid out in the ocean between the king's and queen's realms.

Ed backed out of the room. I copied him. That's just what you do when you're a C student, and the guy sitting next to you gets straight As. Ed had almost six more months of experience with the Seelie side than I did. It didn't matter that he hadn't been brought up in Faerie. It never does when it comes to the queen's rules versus the king's rules. There's such a thing as the home team advantage, but it's really how you play the game that counts. Ed knew this game's rules way better than I did.

Once we were out in the hall, Ed planted his face in his palm.

"What's wrong?" I scratched my head, thinking things had gone pretty well compared to how wrong they could have gone.

"I can't believe we have to find Joyce Watkins."

"What's wrong with that?" I shrugged. "I mean, how hard can it be? If she's an extrahuman, she'll be in the Registry."

"She's in the Registry, all right." Ed shook his head. "The thing is, no one's seen her since just after the Reveal. Joyce didn't even show up when her brother-in-law was in a coma for six months. How's that for missing?" Ed's hands balled into fists, and he stamped his foot. "Fewmets!"

"Now what is it?"

"I can't believe you're not gloating about me asking you another question." He walked away down the hall back the way we had come.

I had nothing to say to that, so I shut my trap and followed him. By the time I got back to the nursery, I realize that I didn't care what Ed owed me anymore. What bothered me the most was what he owed the spider goblin. I had no idea what Tsuchi-whatsis even wanted from people. That would be serious trouble before all of this was over.

CHAPTER EIGHT

Albert

Being back on campus with Gemma was weird. Being back anywhere with her was likewise strange but in a good way. Unfortunately, like most times I entered the campus, the wet towel smacking the back of my eyes got worse. Even with Gemma's air magic still in effect, all those different schools of magic hurt me.

Most people assumed my calm and care equaled reserved or uptight. They thought wrong. What they didn't get was that for me, being part of the magical community meant near-constant pain. The magic in the Under was different, mostly. Faerie magic and use, or faerie creatures, or vamps, or shifters just existing didn't give me a headache, but the spellworks of the magi sure did.

I frowned and then winced. As I tried to smooth out my wrinkling forehead, I pondered what in the courtroom could've kicked my migraine off. Magicpsychic devices often record court proceedings, but those rarely made my headaches this bad. Somebody had been using magic then, against the rules and restrictions inherent to the night court or any court of extrahuman proportions. But who?

With Gino Gitano vanishing into witness protection and Richard Hopewell stuck in the Under due to multiple arrest warrants, I couldn't figure out who would dare cast spells in an extrahuman court of law. All the usual devices to detect such illegal doings hadn't registered.

I tried to watch Headmistress Thurston stride toward the pair of Federal agents, but my eyes kept drifting toward Gemma. I told myself to cut it out; quit staring before she noticed and got angry with me. She'd agreed to meet with me and even seemed amicable to my calling that meeting a date. History told me this didn't mean she'd go quietly.

Nothing about Gemma Toland was quiet or safe. Motherhood hadn't mellowed her either. If anything, she strode more boldly than before. She used to be a literal breath of fresh air. Now my old love whistled like a sword arcing through space and time toward an enemy. I understood now after just one day with Hope. Children have a magnifying effect. How would her influence change me? I had no idea at that point.

Pushing my glasses up my nose, I kept pace but hung back. Story of my life. I could've gone past Gemma and even the headmistress, but I never felt like it was the right time to take the lead. Who was I, anyway? A Seelie knight who needed glasses outside the Under and got headaches every time a magus cast a spell, that's who. I was next to useless in the mortal realm as far as the queen was concerned, except when it came to gathering information.

I hated being Her Majesty's spy because there's so much lying in it. Feeling like everything I heard might become a payment for a favor was no way to live. It definitely was not how to win friends and influence people, but it had been my reality since I'd tithed to the queen all those years ago.

Taking a left to where the FBE agents waited, I thought back to the night we'd graduated from Trout Prep and made our promise. Like everything else between us that vow and the trust at its foundation snapped like a frayed rope. I'd thought for so long that trust was all beyond repair. But as I walked toward the Federal agents whose presence tempted me to come clean, I realized that sharing information with the right people might cost my freedom.

If they threw me in jail, so be it. At least I wouldn't snitch to the queen on the people I loved at Richard's suggestion. I closed my eyes, letting my feet travel ground familiar enough to trod in my sleep. Blaine Harcourt had accused Tony for months of the transgressions I'd been under orders to make. It was about time I paid my dues for membership in the club he'd nearly been expelled from.

"Sir Dunstable," the voice matched the woman seated inside the room better than the man who'd greeted me at its door, but I understood immediately. The werewolf was the good cop in this partnership. "Agent Derek Dennison. And this is Agent Natalie Johnson."

"Hello, Agents." I walked about halfway through the room before my knees knocked like kids out in the cold. Would I make it to a seat before blurting everything out? My composure had been at a breaking point for the last six months and I couldn't take it anymore, not even for the moments required to cross that room.

"Whoa, hold on there, Sir." The rusty staccato of a chair dragged across the floor follow Dennison's voice. The werewolf's viselike grip trapped my arm as he ushered me to the seat. I collapsed into it.

"I did not expect this." Agent Johnson arched her eyebrow in my general direction.

"Good point, partner." Dennison circled me like a shark in bloodied water. His toothy grin spooked me more than the opening scene of Jaws. "I've never seen a Sidhe show fear before."

"Neither have I." Agent Johnson's sunny smile called to mind an avalanche on a ski trail more than a picnic at the beach. "I've got a feeling we're in store for some game-changing intel here."

"What I have to tell you won't change any games." I stared at the floor because I couldn't look either of them in the eye. "All it'll do is confirm that the other side hasn't played by the same rules as you all this time."

"You do understand that if you chat with us now, you are waiving your right to a lawyer?" Agent Johnson's eyebrow reached dizzying heights.

"That's okay." I took a deep breath and released it, counting to five in my head. "I'm almost a lawyer. Anyway, I don't think anyone will want to represent me after I do this."

Agent Dennison stopped his pacing. Flipping a chair around, he sent it backward. The gesture gave me a fleeting moment of comfort, and I closed my eyes around a memory montage of his little brother, Josh Dennison, sitting the same way as he fostered and guided his pack. But Derek was a totally different animal. I caved to the idea that this time, the lawmen were not my allies.

Or maybe they were. I needed to wait and see. Letting all the air out of my lungs, I tried to expel the last remnants of the migraine at the same time. When I took my next breath, I imagined it bracing me, girding my mind to prepare for this figurative battle against my Monarch. Not all wars are lost or won by physical means.

Fred Redford had bested the entire Seelie army with music. I aimed to do the same by wielding the truth.

After I spilled the beans, the agents had me sign a few things and leave with another. I made it to my next social obligation on time, but just barely.

Ed

Back in the nursery, I found a ball and kicked it. Had to watch my mouth around Hope. If I wasn't careful, I'd owe her my life. I didn't want to owe a girl that much when I had work to do. There was a mystery in the queen's court, and I was on the case.

The ball made a hollow pinging sound as it hit the wall and bounced back toward me. I closed my eyes and ducked out of the way, remembering all those forbidden games of dodgeball back when I was at the regular school. That part of my life was over, and I was only seven. All the grown-ups called me an old soul. They didn't understand the half of it.

I shook my head and felt something flying off my face, not my hair. My nose was all stuffed up suddenly too, the stupid thing. I headed toward the bathroom looking down at the pale marble floor and how my shoes almost seemed like they were CGI'd in. I didn't even fit in here in the Under where half my family worked and lived. Down here, I couldn't talk to Rob, who kept me more cheerful than usual. I missed him, which was the story of my life.

I reached one hand out for the bathroom latch. Another one slapped it away. I turned, blinking up at Hertha Harcourt. She took one look at my face, and her flat mouth narrowed into something resembling the letter O. She reached toward my face, but I ducked and headed into the bathroom before she could catch me. At least if somebody had to see me cry, it was the motherly dragon lady instead of that birdbrain, Hope.

I washed my face at the sink, screwing my fists into my eyes to let whatever happened happen. When I got done crying, I flushed the toilet. You can't be too careful about not letting a girl see you cry. As I turned to dry my hands, the water I'd dripped everywhere made me slip. I stumbled into a weird gold planter with a stalk of bamboo sticking out of it and sat down hard on the floor. I'd seen a brownie before.

"That's not bamboo." I spoke at it from the spot on the floor where I sat wincing at my bruised tailbone. A draft of cool air hit the back of my neck.

"Of course not." The pitter-pat of feet smaller than mine echoed from the shower stall behind me. "What are you doing in here anyway, Ed?"

"There's no way you haven't learned what people do in the bathroom." I stood up and brushed off the seat of my pants, hoping nothing icky from the floor stuck to them. "It's not nice to hide in here."

"Well, duh. But I don't like being alone with the dragon lady."

"Bathrooms are for privacy." I shook my head. "Preschool helps with that idea, just saying."

"You big giant jerk." Hope put her hands on her hips. "You know I got home-schooled. Or boat-schooled. Or whatever."

"Hey, Psychic kid, why so surly?" The bamboo bent in my general direction.

"Excuse me?" I put my hands on my hips, frowning at the brownie. I couldn't believe the stick was taking her side.

"Oh, ho ho! A question. I love those." The brownie straightened, something I'd heard was just like a smile for them.

"This sucks." I clenched my fists, digging my fingernails into my palms.

"Yeah, like royally." Hope reached out and patted me on the back. I shrugged her off.

"Yes. Literally even." Hearing a voice from something that looked like a stick was one of the weirdest things I'd seen in Faerie. At least brownies were less creepy than *Tsuchigomo*.

"Literally doesn't mean what you think it means." I shook my head. Being ahead with the verbal skills made me a stick-in-the-mud with kids my own age. Possibly everyone else, too. "What are you, some kind of Millennial brownie?"

"And that's question number two." If the brownie wore any kind of expression, I couldn't tell what it was. "The Redfords are usually better at this game than you seem to be. Are you sure you're Duke Neil's son?"

"Listen, bub," Hope growled and put her hands on her hips,

staring at the pure faerie creature. "You're playing dirty pool. I'm the Alkonost, which means I'm stronger than you, and I won't stand for this. Stop teasing him."

"But it's so easy."

"I could just start asking you questions." Hope tapped her foot, the sound echoing like dripping water on the bathroom tile.

"You probably should if you don't want little Redford here in my debt."

"And why is that?" Hope turned sideways to drop me a wink. I shook my head, but she didn't seem to care.

"Because I have information that no self-respecting faerie would give away for free, so either he pays the price or you do."

"Why should I believe you about knowing stuff?" Instead of tapping her toes this time, Hope practically bounced on them.

"I hear everything that goes on in this castle, you know. We brownies have the bodies for it, after all. Your little Psychic friend there made a deal with the *Tsuchigomo*. I also heard that Ed practically owes you his life already, and I think both of you are way too young for that sort of commitment."

"All that's none of your business." My foot stomped the floor. "I think you have no business in the queen's nursery's bathroom, anyway. The dragon lady isn't going to be happy to learn you've watched her use the can all this time."

"Oh, she knows I'm here." The brownie straightened against the wall. "We've got history, and from what I gather, she rather likes me."

"Well, I don't care whether she likes you or not." I brushed lint off the front of my pants. "I don't like you peeping at us every time we take a leak."

"Relax, Redford, I'm not some kind of pedo. I'm just here doing a favor for someone I can't name."

"Okay, fine. But you'd better turn around every time I come in here to use the toilet for real." I put my hand over my mouth, realizing I'd incriminated myself for crying in here.

"Listen, one of you has to ask me a third question. Kids don't usually do too well in here, especially after what happened to Cosmo. You need my information. Badly."

I blinked at the brownie. They just stood there, of course. Brownies don't have faces to make expressions with. But Hope seemed able to read the brownie's posture and even find tells in their physical stance. Maybe it had something to do with her being a magical shifter. But I was just a medium. Ghosts are my wheelhouse, and what I should have stuck to.

"So, if you want to help us," Hope tilted her head to look sideways at the brownie, " just do it already, with no debt."

"You grew up on an Unseelie pirate ship, so I'll give you this one. Over here in Seelie land, the rules don't bend. Proper payment for favors or information is law. The queen would burn me at, well, *as* the stake if I gave away freebies this big."

"Well, it was worth a try." Hope shrugged. "So who's this Cosmo person?"

"We're in business now." The brownie crackled where I thought their hands might be if they had them. "Cosmo Gitano is the son of Gino and the half-brother of Tony. He's technically about a year old but doesn't look his age. Cosmo's important for the part you kids have to play in all of this. You'll meet him soon."

"Okay." Hope gave the brownie side-eye again. "Go on, buddy."

"Thank you for not calling me 'dude' like our kind have a gender. I hate that." I heard something like the wind rubbing two branches together and realized the brownie laughed. "Anyway, the spider fiend didn't tell you the whole story. He said to find Joyce Watkins but didn't say that you can't actually do that. You need to be in the right place for her to find you."

"Yeah, the whosiwhatsis didn't seem like the friendliest guy in the world." Hope made a spinning gesture with one hand. "Go on."

"The only way to let Joyce find you is to be with her missing husband at the right time," the brownie said. "Otherwise, you'll have to convince her you're who she needs to work with."

"Grown-ups don't believe us, so that sounds like a lost cause." I opened my hand and looked at the palm, stopping short of planting my forehead inside it.

"We'll just have to swoop in and make her listen." Hope grinned. "She'll want to anyway if she's Precognitive."

"You don't know much about being Psychic." I shook my head. "She has to work at seeing the future, not just get the vapors and make predictions just because we show our faces."

"Hey, for all we know, she's already foreseen this and will be expecting us." Hope put her hands on her hips and looked at the brownie. "You can keep talking now."

"You're going to get annoyed at this next part. One of you can't go to find Edgar Watkins."

" I don't know any Edgars. Do you, Ed?"

"Actually, I just found that part out a little while ago." I shivered like a goose walked over my grave. "Edgar Watkins has been hiding in an old junk shop on the East Side. It's called Trash to Treasure, and it's in a warded building over on Camp Street."

"I think that's all the information I've got for you crazy kids." The brownie crackled.

"Thanks, pal." Hope smiled. "I'd say I owe you two, but that wasn't our deal." She shrugged.

"It's okay. You win some, you lose some. And I promise I'll look away whenever either of you uses the toilet."

"You mean when anybody uses it." It was my turn to glare at the brownie.

"Sure, fine, okay, whatever." I managed not to blink in surprise at the brownie's use of my brother's and his friends' inside joke. This stick really did listen in on everything, it seemed.

"It's not cool to mimic a knight of the queen's court." I tapped one foot.

"See?" Hope jabbed me in the ribs with one elbow. "I knew

you'd get the hang of this no-questions game with enough practice. Good job, Ed."

"One more thing." We both waited for the brownie's response. They tilted toward me. "Your brother will have his own problems to deal with soon, but don't let that stop you from going to the queen's ceremony. Something's happening there that you shouldn't miss."

"We'll take that into account, but we're kids." Hope cocked her head to the side.

"Yeah," I nodded, "we're kind of at the mercy of whoever will cart us around."

"Understood." The brownie leaned back against the wall, letting gravity do its job. They looked more like a plain old stalk of bamboo than ever. "I'd tell you to take it easy, but I think that'll be impossible."

"Thanks again." Hope waved at the brownie as I opened the door, letting us both back into the nursery.

Hertha Harcourt stood by the bathroom door doing the pee-pee dance. I stepped out of her way, trying not to laugh as she trotted into the restroom. Hope took the seat the dragon lady had vacated.

Music I never imagined in my wildest dreams came from Hope's mouth. She sang to the egg, some kind of lullaby in a language I didn't recognize. All I could do was stare and let it soothe me until she finished.

"I never heard that song before."

"That's because I just made it up." Hope grinned. "The language, too. Baby dragons in eggs don't really have any language yet, so singing to them in a made-up one makes sense. Besides, baby dragons are special. They deserve something new."

"There's nothing wrong with old." I snapped harder than rubber bands against wrists. I'd become obsessed with the way things used to be, probably because ghosts were my only friends.

"Oh." Hope scratched her head. "I'm sorry."

I watched her face, noticing her eyes tighten and her lower lip tremble. Of course, she wanted to invent things. Her family was just as broken as my own, and her bestie wasn't a Colonial poltergeist. I felt like the biggest jerk in either world, making a littler kid cry like that over something I knew all about. For as long as I could remember, I'd wanted to be like my brother or my dad when I grew up. So why was I on this poor girl's case, sounding exactly like my mom?

"No, Hope. Don't apologize." I sat next to her, but not too close. "I just happen to know that old stuff is as important as the new stuff. It's worth it sometimes to fix the old and broken because then—"

"It's just as good as new." Hope wiped her eyes. "Sorry if I upset you, too. Friends don't hurt each other."

"I'm not upset." I wiped mine too. "Well, not anymore."

The door to the nursery opened, revealing my brother Fred all decked out in his red and white armor like something from a *Game of Thrones* poster, the red baseball cap on his head looking a little ridiculous with the rest of the outfit.

"It's time to go down to the courtyard, you guys." Fred stood to one side in the doorway, holding it open for us. "Come on."

"This is for the queen's shindig down there, I guess." I stood up.

"Yeah. I'd like to say it'll be fun, but I'm not sure."

"Well, I guess we won't know until we go." Hope gave the egg one final friendly pat and followed along behind me.

The toilet flushed from inside the bathroom. That door opened as the hall door closed. I followed my brother and my friend down the hall, with no idea what changes awaited us.

CHAPTER NINE

Albert

I ran all the way from where the portal in the back of the Solarium led. Portals between the Under and the mortal realm were either well established or made spontaneously to a location with people the portal user had a sympathetic connection with. Opening one to a person watching a tithing ceremony was an insult at best.

I knew where I was going, but it took two minutes to get from the portcullis of the castle gate to the central courtyard. My Sidhe magic let me run much faster than any other extrahuman, making up for lost time.

Being in the Under meant that faerie magic didn't give me a headache, which was a good thing considering I'd only just recovered from a blistering one. For a moment, I worried that I might drop the new equipment the Feds had outfitted me with. I shook that idea off. Spider shifter silk stayed put. It'd take a spider shifter or the queen herself to get rid of the stuff.

When I reached the hall leading into the courtyard, I slowed my pace. Stepping under the arch brought me in view of all assembled. I walked at a dignified pace with long strides. Keeping my eyes on the small group gathered to witness what might be one of the most catastrophic event in Seelie history made my vision tunnel-focused. I needed that, or I'd risk panicking and running the other way.

I stopped at the back of the crowd. My rank as a knight entitled me to a closer position, but this gave me a better vantage point. From the top tier of the castle amphitheater, I saw Fred down on the lower level, standing with Ed and Hope. My eyes and mind acknowledged other familiar faces, but they fell by the wayside as I watched the proceedings. The pit of my stomach grew heavy when I saw the thin gold circlet looped over the queen's wrist. She gestured at the Tree and then at Hopewell.

Nobody besides Her Majesty seemed to understand just how strong Richard Hopewell's magic was. I could barely think straight in his presence because of all the different energies he commanded. It was almost as bad as being on campus at Providence Paranormal.

He rivaled three thousand student magi in raw strength. And here the queen was setting him up with a high rank to get heirs, or marry him, or both. Richard Hopewell knelt before Her Majesty without asking her three questions. This departure from custom drew gasps and rigid postures of startlement from the crowd.

But the queen cared about that power, not all the things that made this man dangerous. Hopewell believed in nothing less than magical supremacy, a viewpoint that framed humans akin to animals, with shifters only slightly above that. I didn't want to contemplate the volume of pain and suffering he'd cause if given the chance. The only thing holding him back was the singular limitation each Extramagus had. None of us had figured out what that was yet, but it wouldn't matter once he'd gone full faerie. If he ranked high enough here in the Under to command invading forces, the mortals were toast.

Perhaps the Seelie monarch had understood, had known but thought he'd never get out of hand. She held that gleaming circle above Richard's brow. I'd never seen an accessory like that, not even for a marquess. He murmured something I couldn't hear.

"I prepare now to accept the pledge of one Richard Hopewell, and bind him to my tithe as prince."

Like some massive creature taking a breath, the crowd gasped. Everyone at court knew the Extramagus courted the queen, and that she seemed amenable to his suit, but no one expected her to let him rise above marquess. Declaring a prince or princess was a risk as it was the only rank high enough to challenge either monarch. It meant that Her Majesty saw her suitor as a peer, more than someone to get children with. I headed down the side aisle. The queen was about to make her intended vulnerable one final time before bestowing that vast authority upon him. And I intended to exploit that.

"If there is any courtier present who objects, speak now." The queen gazed over the crowd.

Down in the front row, I watched Ed cover Hope's mouth with one hand. She spluttered around it, and for a moment, I thought the boy would step forward himself. I wouldn't have blamed him, considering the havoc Richard had wreaked on the Redford family, but Fred stopped his kid brother. He lifted one foot to cross the line from spectator to spectacle. I tried to get to it before him but didn't make it in time.

"Your Majesty, I have a grievance against this man." Fred stood, as solid and unwavering as a mountain.

The Redcap's armor gleamed in the sun, edges made sharp and cruel by its light. A harsh-enough complaint might utterly ruin Richard Hopewell, up to and including his immediate death. The Extramagus was guilty of so many things just in the past year, violations so heinous that the queen could do nothing but strike him down if she had proof or a credible witness.

"Then name it, Sir Redford." Hopewell inclined his head in Fred's general direction. His eye twitched.

But a thin and knobbly gray hand wrapped itself in Fred's blood-red tabard before he could speak again. Fred glanced down at the imp, his eyes widening as it mouthed the words, "Remember what you owe me." The retributive fire fueling my peer's hunger for justice snuffed itself like a birthday candle as his honor slew his need for vengeance. Fred addressed the queen, ignoring Richard's interjection.

"He owes my brother an apology, Your Majesty." Fred's alternate grievance deflated the tension halfway. The move was merciful but not entirely benign.

The queen said nothing, just turned to her intended, tilting her head. Richard Hopewell's cheeks took on a reddened splotchiness, as though he rankled at the thought of having to apologize to a mere child. Not everyone present understood that if the Extramagus didn't make things right with the Redfords and mean it, he'd be blocked from tithing in this court altogether.

"I extend my most sincere apology to young Master Redford." Richard Hopewell's voice carried across the crowd, but our perception wasn't important. Neither was Ed's. The only being whose judgment mattered stood eternally in the middle of the courtyard. "I never intended to complicate his life."

The Tree swayed even though no trace of a breeze blew. One branch dipped down until it hung over Richard's head. One set of twigs grown into a u-shape quivered like a tuning fork, as though measuring sounds and tones for the weight of a falsehood. This was the measure of faerie law to the letter, not spirit. The pronged branch withdrew, and the Tree assumed its prior arrangement against the stone and sky.

Gazing up at it, the queen scanned myriad branches—for what, I couldn't tell. She nodded, turning back to the matter and the man at hand. A smile, light as a feather, curled the ends of her lips as roses touched her cheeks. Instead of ethereal, she'd gone earthy. I found her too solidly beautiful, almost as if this queen standing before her court and subjects was a leaden facsimile instead of the real thing. And when she spoke, her voice carried more weight than I was used to hearing in it.

"Rise, Prince Richard."

And he did, in more ways than one. I settled my right cheek into one hand, rubbing my aching temple. Sir Fred stepped back, bending his ear to his brother, Ed. The kid and my daughter explained something to him, both talking with their hands. After that, the group approached me.

I should have known saving the Faerie kingdom couldn't be as simple as one Redcap's defiance. All the same, I did as he asked and brought his kid brother back to the mortal realm right after the illness-inducing ceremony.

If I couldn't be a real hero, at least I'd help one or two. While spying on them for the mortal authorities, of course. If there were a Heaven, I would have asked for its help.

Gemma

When Al went with the Agents, I tagged along behind the Headmistress. At first, I thought she either didn't know or care I followed, but when she got to her office and held the door, she dispelled that illusion.

"Have a seat, Miss Tolland." She gestured at the leather-upholstered chair in front of the desk.

"Thanks." I sat in it, on the edge.

My anticipation of more lessons or being asked to leave within minutes was misplaced. Henrietta Thurston bent at the waist and murmured something at a drawer on her side of the desk. I heard a click and then the sound of metal on wood as she opened and then closed it. The manila folder she'd withdrawn rattled as she opened it.

It contained a yellowed paper with deckled edges bundled together to a photograph by a neon green paperclip. Five teens smiled upside-down out at a world at least forty years older than the one I lived in. One of them was Henrietta herself. I recognized two more as Henry Baxter and Richard Hopewell. But the other two, a dusky-skinned girl with black hair and a pallid bespectacled fellow embracing her, I'd never seen.

"You wonder who they are, of course." The Headmistress tapped the couple with one fingertip. "That's Dahlia and Neil, the couple who shouldn't have gotten together but did, anyway."

"Did it work out?" I gripped the arms of my chair to keep from slapping my hands over my mouth. It felt like a stupid question, even though I figured it made sense to ask.

"Yes, while they lived. But Dahlia died right before the Reveal in a battle against the last Extramagus." Henrietta bowed her head, out of respect or regret, I couldn't tell. "Or what we thought was the last one, anyway."

"Did Neil ever move on from that?" I gazed down at the kid with the James Spader haircut, wondering where he was now.

"No, not truly. We tried all kinds of divination, hoping to find out that a new love was in his cards, though."

"Really? Coincidence usually helps things along. That seems odd." I chewed on my lower lip. I was odd, too, according to my benchmark.

"It's not so strange as you might think. Right after the Reveal, we had to keep our abilities secret. We couldn't rely on chance the way extrahumans do now. And Neil was a master of the rarest school of magic."

"What's that?" I looked up from the photo, then away from Henrietta's eyes and the tears in them.

"Null. It's basically anti-magic."

"Wow." I swallowed around the lump forming in my throat, sensing an unhappy ending to go with this tale.

"Yeah. He was the only reason a handful of kids stood any

chance of going up against an Extramagus." She unclipped the photo, turning it around so I could see it better.

"Well, and you had another one with you all along." I pointed at Richard's smirking face.

"But we didn't know that's what he was. Memory wipes convinced us that his fire magic was incredibly strong, rivaling a dragon's." She closed the folder, obscuring her and Richard so only Dahlia and Neil remained visible. "Because of Neil's headaches, you see."

"Headaches?" I bent down, looking more closely at the boy with the glasses. He had an all-too-familiar line between his eyes.

"Yes. One of two things Null magi have in common."

"What's the other one?" I already knew the answer to that question, plain as the spectacles on Neil's face.

"Nearsightedness." The headmistress cocked her head to one side, as though listening for something. Her nostrils flared.

"Great Goblin King's Garters!" I stood up. Those two things were intimately familiar, for good reason.

"Heh." She gave me a half-smile and opened the folder again. "The old Watkins adage rings true. You know more than you think you know." Henrietta addressed the door this time. "You can come in."

The door swung out on silent hinges. I turned to see Henry Baxter, who looked almost the same as he had in the photo on the desk, just paler. He held something hidden in one hand. Beside him stood a girl who I couldn't place. Had I seen her before?

"Good," said Henrietta. "You brought Maddie."

I looked back at the headmistress and blinked. What had she just said? I scratched my head and then spied the photo again. The girl in the photo, Dahlia. She reminded me of someone. But who?

"Um, something funny's going on around here." I narrowed my eyes, then turned and almost jumped out of my seat. "Who's this girl? She wasn't here a second ago."

"Oops." She shrugged and smiled, then touched her necklace and murmured something at it. "Sorry about that. No more reruns now. I'm Maddie, Umbral magus."

"Oh, okay." I nodded. I'd learned about Umbral magic during the first hour of intensives with the headmistress.

"What have you got for me, Henry?" Headmistress Thurston tilted her head to peer at whatever the vampire gripped.

"It's the best I can do." He clenched his fingers over the object and sighed. "I've been through the entire box of memory trinkets, and this one's the closest I can get to an answer that fits your theory."

"Even if you'd found nothing, I still believe we're part of a deliberate pattern here." She leaned forward, hands against the desk.

"Deliberate?" I blinked. "You mean to tell me you've had the idea all along that all this chaos, well, isn't chaotic at all?"

"It's always been at the back of my head. It has felt familiar ever since last fall, but I haven't been able to put my finger on it." Henrietta held her hand out, palm up, toward Henry. "Let's see this thing."

The vampire opened his hand, revealing an old keychain. It had one of those rings that detached by pulling away from a round plastic base. The time-worn words Trash to Treasure crossed the circle at its equator, with a Providence address beneath it that didn't exist. The headmistress put her palm over it, then tapped her foot.

"Okay." Henry bowed his head, looking wearier than I imagined a member of the blood-drinking set could get. He murmured something.

Headmistress Thurston's eyes went wide, and her mouth dropped open. The next moment, her lips pressed into a thin, pale line. A low growl grew in the silence, eventually filling the room. She held her free hand out, and a ball of foxfire, blue and shot through with crackles of static electricity, floated above it. Inside, a scene took shape.

"Nobody will find you, Uncle Edgar." The Neil in this image looked older and more careworn, with dark purple circles under his eyes and a leaner face. Gray streaked his honey-blond hair.

"Are you sure?" The man who spoke had covered his bald head with a Greek fisherman's cap.

"The wards I put up should hold indefinitely. Even after I'm—"

"They got all kinds of new treatments with magipsychic meds now." The man I could only assume was Edgar Watkins shook his head. "You're not dying, kid."

"This leukemia sucks rotten eggs, but I've had it longer than those new trials allow." Neil cleared his throat. "And I'm not a kid anymore. My part in this is almost done. It'll be up to Henrietta and her friends from the future or whatever Aunt Joyce saw."

"Right." Edgar turned his head to the side, rubbing one eye. "All you need to do now is—"

"Hide Joyce. I know. And then I can rest." He cleared his throat again, then coughed twice and wiped his mouth. His hand came away with blood on it.

"Jeez, kid. Go to the hospital first." Edgar shuffled his feet.

"You know I can't." Neil popped a Halls lozenge into his mouth. "But I promise I will right after. With great anti-power comes great responsibility and all that."

"Wish I could visit you." Edgar fussed with his hat, trying to hide the tears at the corners of his eyes.

"No matter what happens, don't." Neil pushed his glasses up the bridge of his nose. "That goes double for Henry, and triple for Aunt Joyce."

"I know." Edgar sighed. "Direct interaction will break the Nullification spell. I still don't get why we can't tell the other guy what he's in for."

"She said there was a good reason he can't know what he is until the last minute." Neil pulled a light jacket on.

"Yeah. That's my Precognitive wife, always right." Edgar gave his nephew a thin smile. "See you around, kid."

"Thanks, Uncle Edgar." Neil's back was to his uncle now, but everyone watching the memory saw the tears streaming down his face.

"For what?" Edgar reached one hand out but then let it drop to his side.

"Taking me in when I had nowhere else to go. You saved my life back then. It's my privilege now to save yours."

"I wouldn't have had it any other way, kid."

The scene faded, replaced by the blazing blue Foxfire. I dabbed my nose with the hankie I usually kept up my sleeve. The sniffling from off to my right told me that Maddie May also grieved a man she hadn't known. Both the headmistress and Henry Baxter stood in the middle of the office, ugly-crying. From Neil's last remaining high school besties, I should have expected nothing less.

CHAPTER TEN

Ed

"Sir Al, I'm not sure you brought me to the right place." I peered up at the Sidhe knight. I saw his resemblance to Hope from this angle. The stubborn streak, too. "I need to meet Lane Meyer, not hang out in my warded room."

"I didn't want to take any chances by just dropping you at their studio." He unfolded the glasses he always wore in the mortal realm and perched them on his nose like a weird, wiry bird.

"I've been there before." Shrugging, I leaned against the wall.

"So have I." Al nodded once. "And Goblins can tell if you've returned to old haunts with a simple spell."

"The king has no problem with me; just saying. Anyway, he can get in here easy on account of my dad."

"It's not the king I'm worried about."

"I'd like to know who's threatening me if it's all the same to you."

"All I'm allowed to tell you is that it's a Seelie Goblin."

"Oh." I scratched my head. "Wait. Aha, I figured it out! The

Harcourts' old butler. Kim said Blaine thought he let the Pharaoh's rats into the mansion."

"I'd say you ought to be out solving the city's little mysteries if I weren't concerned for your safety." A muscle in his jaw twitched.

I wondered whether he worried more about Hope's safety because she was my friend, but I figured it didn't matter. Someone watching my back for a selfish reason was better than no one at all.

"Thanks for caring." I tugged his sleeve, so he'd look me in the eye and see I wasn't being flip. I'd already solved a mystery; a dangerous one, too, but Al didn't need to know about that. Just like his daughter, he needed a friend. "Seriously. I feel neglected by the adult solids in my life lately."

"Are you sure you're only six?" One corner of his mouth turned up.

"Seven. Almost." I mirrored his half-smile. "Anyway, I'm supposed to meet with Lane."

"All right." Albert Dunstable pulled his phone from his jacket and tapped. "There, I pressed Send."

"It's so weird, being over there at the queen's castle where it's broad daylight but still night here." I stared out the window at the moon.

"You get used to it." Al tilted his head so his ear pointed at the window. "You'll want to get that."

"Okay." I didn't bother wondering how he knew Lane was already here. Sidhe have excellent hearing.

Heading downstairs to invite a vampire in, I literally ran into and through Rob. He laughed and sailed behind me as I kept moving. Mediums, that is, Psychics who'd either almost or actually died for a minute, worked with a ghostly partner. Rob's my ghost. Has been for as long as I can remember.

"How's my best solid buddy today?" He tipped his tricorn hat.

"Okay." I shrugged one shoulder.

"That's what you always say."

"Yeah."

"The Under's rubbing off on you, kid." Rob shook his head. "It's safe to ask me stuff, you know?"

"Yeah, but there's no time." I'd reached the bottom of the stairs and glimpsed Lane's green hair even through the semi-sheer curtain over the door. Mama had put them up over the summer. My thoughts turned toward my mother before I could stop them. Of course, Rob sensed that.

"She's fine, kid." He sighed. "I checked and everything."

"I don't care," I lied. "Gotta let Lane in now."

"Listen, let me follow you." Rob stood in the door, his face and toes sticking out from the wood, along with his portly belly. Yup, my ghost had a dad-bod. "Just while you're here. Let me out of the wards when you go, please?"

"Sure." I nodded, then looked Rob in the eye and thought hard at him about how I wanted him to keep an eye on Al instead of me. We'd done the Possession thing so many times, Rob could hear my thoughts as long as he was within arm's length.

"I'll watch what I want but I get what you mean, kid." Rob moved aside as I reached for the doorknob. It was a hexagon that reminded me again of the stupid soul-spindle and the trouble it had caused for Mama and Professor Watkins, all because she'd teamed up with a ghost on Richard Hopewell's side by accident.

"Hey, Rob?" I looked up into his doughy face.

"Yeah?"

"Thanks for picking me back in the day."

"Oh. Um, you're welcome." He sailed out the door, then through me and up the stairs.

Rob always held something back. He'd never told me how or why he'd partnered with a tiny tot, only that it was a long story, and he'd get around to it someday. All the someday stuff sucked. It wasn't doing people my parents' age any good, and it looked like the college kids were falling into the same trap. I'd have to give them a few reminders right when they needed it. I started by opening the door.

"Hey, Lane."

"Hey, yourself, kiddo." Lane smiled. He always did that around me because he knows vampire fangs aren't scary when you can talk to ghosts.

"You can come in." I pulled the door wide.

"Wow." Lane blinked. "Is your dad okay with that?"

"It doesn't matter now." Standing aside, I let him in, then closed the door. "I need to talk to you before we head out." I walked toward the kitchen, straight into the pantry.

Pointing at the chain above my head, I made as much room as possible for the vampire to get in there with me before he pulled it. After that, I ducked under his arm and shut the door behind us. I grabbed the can of Spam that wasn't full of mystery meat product and said the words to activate the magipsychic sound-proofing device Headmistress Thurston had given me, just in case.

"Okay, this only lasts a minute, so I have to talk fast."

"Yup." Lane nodded, which meant that, even if he wasn't cool with being shut in a closet with his best friend's kid brother, he could at least handle my paranoia.

"Something's off with Sir Al. He's acting less formal and seems jumpy. Same goes for Rob. I don't trust them to let me do my thing, and I'm on a Quest."

"Okay, so the parental wannabes are dropping the ball on you. I get it. But why tell me?"

"Because you're my getaway Summoner. You've got to tell Al that the place we're going won't let Seelies in or something. I already asked Rob to follow Al for me, so that's set."

"Does Fred know about this?" Lane tugged one ear.

"Here." I handed him the scrap of parchment where my brother had scrawled "trust the kid" with Hope's old crayon stub.

Lane nodded. "So, what are we actually doing?"

"You'll find out after they're gone." The can beeped. "We're out of time."

I opened the door, pointed at the chain, and put the Spam back. Lane walked out and I followed, snagging a box of animal crackers off another shelf as I went. Good thing, too. Al had just come down the stairs, looking puzzled until he spied the cookies.

"Are you allowed to eat those this late at night?" Al pointed at my snack.

"I'm hungry. Didn't get to stay for the queen's lunch thingamabob."

"This must be like jet lag for you, whether dessert at this hour is strictly in the rules."

I didn't answer, only looked at Lane.

"Al, we've got a problem. The place we've gotta go is strictly nocturnal—"

"Understood." Al nodded. "I've got an errand I can run, anyway." He headed toward the door. Over his shoulder, he added, "Bring your ghost friend."

"Sure," I fibbed again.

Lying to a friend's dad bugged me, even though it had to be done. Al headed out the door, and Rob sailed after him, unseen. Lane glanced at the kitchen clock and tapped his foot in time with the second hand. He gave Al a full minute before heading out and beckoning me to follow. He walked me around the corner and half a block down Camp Street before I spoke.

"So, where are we headed?"

"We're here already." Lane pointed at the space between two clapboard triple-decker buildings. Both looked old and uncared for, like the basement corner where you throw things you don't have time to sort through.

One of them had a porch complete with a grungy rocking chair and the other a small storefront. Looking up, I realized I wasn't looking at two buildings. The third floor on one and the fourth on the other joined above the narrow driveway. The longer I looked at them, the newer they looked, as though my eyes cleaned and polished the buildings, or possibly wiped away layers of Psychic impressions.

"Woah." Lane pushed the hair out of his eyes. "Henry said it'd be weird, but I wasn't prepared for this. Okay, so do you know which one we want for your Quest?"

"I'm not sure, actually." Running up the steps in front of the store window, I peered inside. I expected to see layers of dust or drop cloths over everything, but the stuff inside was clean. There wasn't a sign out front, and the windows were too dingy for shoppers, but I saw the name of the place over the register. "Trash to Treasure. You ever hear of it before, Lane?"

"A couple-few months ago. And then tonight." The vampire held up a battered old keychain with the shop's name. "It looks closed, so come over here and ring the bell, okay?"

We walked to the porch on the other side of the building. I didn't see the bell at first because I expected a button. Instead, it was a rope next to the door, hanging just high enough that I had to stand on my tiptoes to reach it. It jangled inside. After a minute, someone shuffled up behind the front door.

"Wait a minute." The muffled voice sounded off somehow, even through the door. When it creaked open, the man who stood in the narrow space between door and jamb was smaller than I'd imagined. He had the same nose and chin as his brother, Professor Watkins, but those were the only features they shared.

"You're Edgar Watkins?" I didn't have to tilt my head up much to look him in the eye. The black fisherman's cap perched on a bald head where I'd expected hair, and one corner of his mouth drooped in a smirk he probably didn't mean.

"Ayup, son. In the flesh, what's left of it." He nodded at Lane. "You're the Meyer boy. Knew you were coming, both of you." Nate turned watery blue eyes back to my face. "Your ghost off doing what you ordered him to?" He didn't wait for my answer. "That's good. Come in. I'm sick of standing around here."

Watkins let go of the door and turned, one hand on the left wall. His feet shuffled, and I noticed that the floor was bare, the polish on the wood nearly worn away. The entry hall opened into a double parlor, but the old guy didn't cross it. Instead, he lowered himself into a chair only inches away from where the hall ended. Seats of all kinds dotted the entire area like islands on the bay.

Stools, folding chairs, office chairs with wheels, even one high-backed club chair near an empty and cold fireplace. You could chart courses by them, like Edgar Watkins didn't get around too well and had to sit down every so often. Or he used them to hold onto, like he'd done with the wall. Lines of chairs stretched to the kitchen, a back hall, the bathroom. He didn't give me time to figure it out or ask about it.

"I know why you're here, son." He took a few shallow breaths. "And I want to help you find the box, but I can't. Not now."

"It's okay." I shrugged. "It's gotta be in the store. Just let me in, and I'll—"

"It's not that simple." Watkins rummaged in his pocket and pulled out an inhaler. He shook it, held it to his ear, and hung his head. "I don't know where the Sprite hid it, you see." The old man coughed so hard I could swear he left his body for a few seconds.

"Where do you keep them?" Lane held out his hand. "I'll get you another."

"Last one."

"What?"

"Don't matter. Won't need it much longer. We wait."

I would have asked who or what he meant, but Edgar coughed. He didn't stop for such a long time I thought Lane might call 911. Instead, he sent a text. We waited, like the man told us. In the kitchen, I ran water into a chipped coffee mug. Lane picked up an old ukulele and strummed, then made a sour face and tuned it. Edgar sipped water from the mug.

"Kid!" Rob flailed his translucent arms outside the front

window. "Al dropped a paper in the college library and went poof —ported out. And some lady's out here—"

The doorknob turned.

"Joyce." A smile to shame the sun rose on Edgar Watkins' face. The corners of his eyes glimmered with an oasis of tears.

"Eddie!" A whip-thin woman in better health but about the same age as Edgar rushed to his side. "I've missed you so much."

"We have little time." Edgar leaned closer, reaching up and putting his hands on either side of Joyce's face. She hugged him. He whispered something in her ear.

Lane sat up, green eyes going wide. He looked pale, even for a vampire. His mouth dropped open, showing his fangs. I couldn't do anything but sit there, even though I felt the shiver at the back of my neck that meant death was near.

"Oh, no, Eddie—" Joyce's voice got thicker than a stack of encyclopedias, heavy with knowledge. She had to be Psychic, like Lane and me, and either a Telepath or Precog.

The energy in the room built toward what I knew would be its awful conclusion. Edgar took one too-short breath, then another. It rattled out, and after that, he breathed no more. Lane shook his head and tapped the left side of his chest to signal that the old man's heart had stopped, too.

"All right, boys." Joyce lowered Edgar's body against the back of the chair, then closed his eyes. She wiped tears from her own. "I have to get the last pieces right. There's work to do and not much time."

"Work?" Lane narrowed his eyes. "What kind of work?"

"Nothing too impossible." Joyce took the phone off the wall and dialed. "Only an adventure in an old rummage shop. And saving the world."

When she finished speaking to the coroner, Joyce hung up and beckoned us upstairs. We followed her up and through a windowless hallway, emerging in another stairwell. The air in here felt different—haunted, even to a medium like me.

Downstairs the shop felt as cluttered as it looked. Aisles almost too narrow to browse comfortably warred with deceptive spaces where crates squatted on otherwise open stretches of floor. Lane picked his way toward some cases full of vinyl records. I held my hands behind my back, understanding that I wasn't powerful enough to handle any trinket or bauble that might lead to a ghost.

Joyce sailed through the shop like her last visit had happened only yesterday. Her mouth moved along with one index finger that pointed out each item. What her movements lacked in speed, they made up in efficiency. Within minutes, she found it—the carved wooden box from my Quest.

Joyce tucked it in a mesh bag, the kind they used at the farmer's market down in Lippitt Park. After that, she left the conjoined houses, looking back once. She took us with her.

Her first stop was to see Tony Gitano and Olivia Adler at the Nocturnal Lounge. She had Lane call Margot Malone to meet us. Once the new arrivals joined us, Joyce marched down to the dorm basement, where Agent Derek Dennison and his partner Agent Johnson waited.

When she told us that Richard Hopewell's magic only worked in Rhode Island, the agents knew exactly what to do. The Feds made rapid travel arrangements and the shifters sent texts, but without Joyce and me, they couldn't have timed it right.

"You make sure the ghosts are on both sides to reinforce the sympathetic connection." Agent Johnson tapped her nails on the table. "That's the only way the Summoners can get one strong enough so the portal goes to the right places."

"Are you sure Ed can do that alone?" Olivia blinked at me.

"I can." I didn't wait for anyone else to defend my abilities. "Horace won't miss the chance to see Bianca again, even if it's just for a few seconds through a portal."

"And you think you can get the rest of them to Swan Point,

Tony?" Joyce pushed a list of names on yellowed paper across the table.

"Yeah. I set it up so we meet Irina first. If one of them gives me trouble, her fiddle will change their mind." Tony's smile differed from the way it used to be. It seemed brighter somehow; less shadowy, like he believed he could do anything now. I caught it. "Olivia and I will go through with you, kid. You won't be alone."

Maybe Joyce was right. Maybe we could save the day.

CHAPTER ELEVEN

Hope

I hated having to go back to the nursery alone. Well, without Ed anyway. Instead, I went with the dragon lady and her egg. It was easy to slip away from them and down the hall. That lady only had eyes for her little baby, and the egg had no eyes to see me with.

I got to the door of unfriendly spider-man's room—Toochie whatever. If I could bargain with the old geezer, maybe Ed wouldn't have to owe anything. He had to see the sense in letting a medium off the hook to get a favor from one of the three magic bird shifters. I tried to knock, but the door opened, and I almost hit the big kid in the face.

"Um, sorry." I stepped back to let the kid go by, but he stood there staring at my wings.

"You're Hope Tolland, the Alkonost."

"Yeah." I twirled one finger. "Big whoop."

"I'm Cosmo. Wow, your wings are something else. Everyone told me about them, but I never thought they'd look so cool."

"Wait, the only Cosmo around here is supposed to be a baby, I thought. But you look like you're ten."

"Well, I'm not even a year old. My mom had the *Tsuchigomo* age me because she gets visions and stuff. And they gave me this." He pulled a crystal on a chain out of his shirt. It looked a lot like the one Hertha wore to keep her from dragoning out.

"It's a bad idea to go around the Under telling random people everything about yourself, you know." I squinted at the crystal, trying to see what animal form it kept good old Cosmo from turning into.

"You're not random. I'm supposed to tell you. Mom said so, and she's Precognitive, from an old family of seers."

"Well, if it's okay with your mom, I guess it's fine with me." I shrugged. "But we're in the hall. Anyone could hear."

"Come in, then." He made room for me to get by.

"But then the Tootsie—Tsuitchy—" I rolled my eyes.

"*Tsuchigomo*." Cosmo grinned. The jerk.

"Yeah, that guy. He'll listen in."

"He's okay."

"But I thought he eats kids."

"Not really." He shrugged. "I'm okay, anyway."

"But he's still super dangerous. He gets favors if you ask him questions, just like a faerie but without the iron allergies."

"Look, he's helping my mom." Cosmo waved a hand at the open door. "He knows her family from way back."

"Okay, then."

We walked into the spider man's room together. Dad would have yelled at me, but I think Mama would have understood. It was a matter of honor at that point, for Ed because I was there to rescue him behind his back and for Cosmo. He was bigger than me, sure, but way younger. My mother always told me I should stick up for younger kids no matter what, even if I might get hurt.

The old spider guy wasn't in the front room. I figured he must be back through that webbed doorway I'd seen the last time with Ed. I sat down at a small table across from Cosmo. The chairs were cushiony and too big for us, so he sat back with his feet sticking out and looking like a goofball. I leaned forward, wishing my toes touched the floor.

"So, I'm figuring the enemy you mentioned is that Hopewell guy who just became the clown prince." I winked, but the kid didn't think my joke was funny. Or maybe he didn't get it.

"That's not set in stone just yet, but he could be." Cosmo shrugged. "And maybe it's you, Hope."

"If I'm fated to be your enemy, it makes no sense for you to talk to me."

"Except that this conversation decides it." Cosmo sat there grinning and swinging his feet.

"Let me guess." I leaned my chin on one hand. "Your mama said so."

"Exactly." Cosmo tapped his nose.

"Hey, I don't even want any enemies. I only came to see—" I waved my hand at the door on the other side of the room. "Him. The old guy."

"*Tsuchigomo*. It's not that hard to say if you practice." He leaned forward and whispered. "I'm gonna take a big chance here. Why do you want to see him?"

"Woah." I blinked. Cosmo had seemed to have the hang of the whole not-asking-questions thing even though he was still a baby. Sort of. "Um, you ask two more, and you'll owe me."

"I know." Cosmo grinned.

"Okay. I want to see the *Tsuchigomo* because I want to buy Ed Redford's debt from him."

"You can try it, but he won't make that deal, not in a zillion years."

"I'll just offer the same thing in exchange. Should work. Alkonost beats medium like scissors beats paper."

"Most of the time, but not to a *Tsuchigomo*."

"I don't get it. For a faerie creature, especially on the Seelie side, it should be a no-brainer."

"He's only sort of a faerie creature, though. He's stuck here until he gets what he needs to leave."

"Hmm. This is hard." I scratched my head. "It can't hurt to offer, I guess."

"You just don't know much about the *Tsuchigomo*, that's all. He needs to collect a bunch of abilities, all at the same time, in order to leave."

"But I can see and hear ghosts. Talk to them, too, just like Ed."

"Mediums can do more stuff you can't, though. Still, he might want something from you all the same. You're right, it can't hurt to try." He grinned. "So go ahead."

I nodded and got out of my chair, looking around. Cosmo just sat there, smirking. I almost headed toward the doorway at the back of the room, but a flutter in the pit of my stomach told me not to. Instead, I looked up.

"Good evening." The big old Tsuchigomo hung upside-down from the ceiling.

"I didn't know you were part bat." I flapped a few times, pulling air through my feathers to get up to his level and look him in the eye. One thick strand of web hung there, looking like a rope swing. He nodded at it, so I perched.

The Tsuchigomo giggled, almost like he was another kid. His hair had new streaks of black in it, and his face looked less wrinkly than the last time I'd seen him with Ed. I turned my head and shut the eye that wasn't pointed at him.

"You seem younger." I chewed my lip. What Cosmo had said made sense. "Yeah, I get it now. You don't eat kids. You drink our youth away, like a vampire with blood."

"Good." The Tsuchigomo nodded. "I need the years from the young medium, as he promised."

"Well, I bet you want some from me, too. You can have mine if you let Ed go. I'll get a boatload more than he ever will."

"My deal with your friend is set, and I cannot cancel it. Doing so would break a promise I made to another."

"Oh."

"But I will make one concession for you. If you give me some of your years, I will take fewer of them from young Master Redford."

"Okay." I nodded.

"You know what you must do to close our deal, young Alkonost."

"Why did the queen make Dick Hopewell a prince?"

"So she could wed him and beget an heir with him."

"Why does Dick want a baby?"

"He does not. He's already got enough power to change life as we know it in the mortal realm, but it's restricted. Not so if he seizes a monarchy, something he will do at his first chance."

I couldn't think of another question to ask. I closed my eyes, trying to decide. What would Mama ask? Nothing. She'd stick a cutlass in the *Tsuchigomo* and call it a night. What would my dad ask? I had no clue. I opened my eyes and my mouth and let the first words in it come out.

"Will the good guys win?"

"I can't answer that question, but someone here and in my debt can." The Tsuchigomo snapped his fingers.

I heard a rustle of fabric, then Cosmo happily clapped his hands. Looking down, I watched an old woman step out of the curtained doorway. She had a head of white curls, except for one lock of black at the right side of her head.

"Mom! Be careful!" Cosmo got up and helped the woman. He gave her his own seat.

"Huh." I'd overheard Miss Olivia and Miss Kim talking about this lady in the summer on Mama's ship. "Cassandra Spanos. She sees the future."

"Yes. And she'll answer your question as payment for her last debt."

"The Extramagus will prevail unless dusk and dawn unite."

"I don't get it." I twisted the webbing I sat on. "That makes no sense. Sunrise and sunset are opposites. They can't ever happen at the same time."

"All the same, that is the truthful answer you have been given." The *Tsuchigomo* waved one hand at me like he was shooing a fly. "Now get out of my webs, young Alkonost. I have other guests to entertain."

I opened my mouth, ready to argue with him, offer him a hundred years of my life if he'd only talk like a regular person instead of a fortune cookie. But before I could say that, the door swung in, busted open by Hertha Harcourt's booted foot. I flew down, ready to protect Cosmo and his mom if I had to.

"Nobu!" She stopped beneath the *Tsuchigomo*, glaring up at him. "I need you!"

Hertha held the egg in her arms, clutching it like Mama gripped the wheel in a rip current. I blinked, noticing the web of cracks all along one side. Something moved in there, something pink and white, but it pushed slowly and with little force.

"Half a moment." The *Tsuchigomo*'s back legs pressed together around a web strand. He came down from the ceiling fast enough to scare me and slow enough that he seemed to float. "Ah, yes. I see. The baby dragon is dying. There's nothing I can do for your child, Hertha. Not until they hatch."

"No!" I rushed forward. The baby couldn't die, not now, when it didn't even get a chance to live yet. "It's not fair."

I reached out, fingers stretched toward the egg. Nobody stopped me, or even made a sound. It was like time or everyone else in that room had stopped except for me and the baby who was so not ready to be born that he or she would die.

But time hadn't stopped. I heard them all breathing, and felt their eyes on my back, my face, my wings. It was like they expected me to do something about this. Me, an almost six-year-old kid who missed her Mama was supposed to save a life like some kind of hero. Or some kind of mythical creature even more powerful than a dragon.

I hadn't learned much about the mystic birds, what the differences were between what Miss Olivia and me were, or about the third feather, either. All I knew was that, even though I didn't know what I could do, that flutter in my stomach told me I should do more than stand there.

Reaching out with my hands and my wings, I took the egg out of Hertha's arms. She let me do it, too; just opened her arms. It seemed like the right thing, and I kept on letting my heart get out in front and lead, like the fastest kid in a race. And what my heart held more of than anything else just then was love.

Folding my wings around so they blocked everyone else in the room was easy. They shut us in together, me and the egg. Inside the wings shut up in Nobu's room closed up in the queen's castle hidden away in her demesne in the middle of the Under. Maybe I was a character in one of those songs about the hole in the bottom of the sea or the old lady who swallowed a fly.

Or those Russian dolls, the ones Father talked about before he died.

I blinked. The thought was so tiny and quiet, it could have come from a Gnome's eyelash. Had the egg talked?

Yes.

What's your name?

Saya. At least, that's what Mother and Brother think at me.

How do you get out of there?

I need to be stronger.

I'll do my best, Saya.

I tried staring at the egg, then tried hugging it and kissing it. Nothing worked, and Saya's movements were fewer as time ticked by. All the breath got knocked out of me, like the time I fell off the main mast. After that, air came in like a lion and out with tears. Those fell on the egg, and still nothing happened. I took another breath and let it out with what I thought would be a tantrum-worthy wail. It wasn't.

Instead, my voice transformed, rising in sadness. It sounded like shifters changing into their animal forms, different but somehow as right as a sunrise. I didn't shriek or cry—I sang.

The words pouring from my mouth came from a memory that didn't belong to me. It was like putting on Mama's shoes or wearing Grandpa's hat. The tune and the words weren't mine. I'd borrowed them from all the other Alkonosts who'd picked up that feather before me. I kept on singing until the song belonged to me, too, and remembered Saya stuck in the egg that whole time. I sent the song in there with her.

Under all the singing was something sharp, another sound. It wasn't a beat, more like maracas or those wooden shells dancers clack together, but it followed along in time with my music. Something strong pressed on my arms, too.

Saya?

Almost.

I answered with my voice, singing louder. My wings opened as though they couldn't stay folded and hold all the sound in anymore. I raised my head, belting out one last, long note. It ended with one more crack. Bits and pieces of eggshell rattled to the floor. But the baby dragon didn't move in my arms.

"Saya?" I looked up at the closest person, who turned out to be Nobu. "She's breathing, but only a little."

"It's my turn." The *Tsuchigomo* held his human arms out. When he tried taking Saya from me, I couldn't let go. I knew it wasn't right to leave her alone. "Very well. I will save the little one and collect my debt from the Alkonost at the same time."

Something as smooth and clean as freshly aired bedsheets but as strong as sailcloth wrapped around Saya and me both. I looked down to see Nobu's spider legs producing silken threads and binding the two of us. I yawned and shut my eyes, sleepy even though I'd had more than enough rest. The last thing I remembered about Nobu's room was my breath and my heartbeat echoing and blending with Saya's until I couldn't tell them apart.

CHAPTER TWELVE

Albert

I put the letter with my apology on top of the card catalog and asked the helper ghosts to deliver it to Headmistress Thurston. Turning to leave, I nearly collided with Taki Waban. The ancient indigenous ice dragon had, for whatever reason, decided to work as the College librarian.

"You must go now." His face wore a wild-eyed and desperate look instead of its usual sleepy grin.

"I was leaving, sir." I resisted the urge to salute such an ancient and dignified creature.

"That's not what I mean." His attention lost focus as though he hearkened to something I couldn't sense. "Dragons, important ones, are in terrible danger, young Knight. Only you can reach them in time."

"Uh—" I blinked. "In the Under? But my connections to dragons aren't strong enough." Without a sympathetic connection, it'd take me hours to track them down.

"They're with your daughter, Knight." His eyes fixed on my face, narrowing focus so tightly it could have skewered me.

"Right." It didn't get much more sympathetic than a blood relation.

I closed my eyes, conjuring an image of Hope behind my eyelids. The corners of my mouth turned up as I imagined her hanging upside-down from a tree branch. Gathering my faerie energy into one hand, I pointed. The sound of Mr. Waban's footsteps as he got out of the way didn't distract my focus. I willed myself to my daughter's side, and there I was, back in the Under.

The room I stood in wasn't the nursery. A cocoon of spider silk exactly the right size to contain a child quivered in the middle of the room. With fists clenched and nostrils flared, I prepared to give Nobu hell for what he'd done to my daughter. A frail and slender hand, crisscrossed with blue veins and powdery wrinkles, pressed my right arm.

"There's no time for an outburst, Sir Dunstable." The dry voice sounded familiar from the College.

I turned my head to peer into the unnaturally wizened face of Cassandra Spanos. She'd traded years of her life to Nobu, and at first, I couldn't fathom why. Then, I beheld the boy at her side. He could only be the yearling son of the big-cat Mafia boss, artificially aged ten years.

I understood Cassandra's bargain at once—a sacrifice for her son's survival. The boy pointed at the pale-blue and green shards littering the floor beside a pair of poison-green Louboutins. Hertha Harcourt.

"But if the egg hatched, where—" I caught myself before asking a question. "The whelpling was premature."

Hertha just nodded. One hand clutched the beribboned collar of her blouse while the other hugged her waist. She gazed at the cocoon, and I understood that the *Tsuchigomo* was taking years from two children, not one.

"Saya is her name, and the Alkonost saved her life." The boy leaned forward and scooped up some eggshells using a scrap of fabric. He handed them to Hertha, who tucked them in her handbag.

"So, the baby is a full-blood female dragon." I peered at the cocoon, imagining what it must be like for my exuberant child to be trapped in with an infant.

"The first in several centuries." Nobu the *Tsuchigomo* untethered the silk strands connecting his body to the cocoon. "And not out of danger yet, according to my Precognitive friend."

I shook off Cassandra's hand, not wanting her Psychic energy interfering with my second portal in mere minutes. My temples ached, and a painful pressure squeezed the back of my head. I knew what, or rather who, was coming.

"Be prepared to flee." The frail Psychic turned to face the door, squaring her shoulders and forcing me to step a few inches farther into the room.

Pushing past the pain was the easy part. I opened my mouth to give them instructions, wanting them all to go through, but I couldn't choke out more than one single syllable.

"Go."

A way back to the Providence Paranormal College Campus opened. With inhuman strength, Hertha hefted the cocoon and bolted out of the Under just as the door from the hallway swung inward, knocking Cassandra to the floor. The boy dropped to his knees, hands outstretched toward his mother.

"You too, Cosmo." The young-old Precog waved her hand like a hankie out a train window in a black and white movie. "I love you."

"But Mom—"

A chuckle like tearing fabric came from the doorway. I didn't have to turn to know Richard Hopewell stood in it. My headache was more than enough confirmation, but there was also a blast of heat as hot as the heart of a bonfire—Spectral magic mingled with plain old fire.

"No!" Nobu held up one hand like a cop at a four-way intersection. "I'm a valuable hostage, and these are my rooms."

"I outstrip your usefulness now, old man." Richard stepped past me like I was part of the furniture. "I'm the prince. If I want to burn everything in here, I will. Starting with them."

He pointed one flame-coated and glowing finger at Cassandra and her son. She sat up, using her momentum to push Cosmo toward my portal. With a sob, he went, tears streaming from his eyes in his wake, but they'd moved too late. Richard's blast was in motion, and it'd catch them.

I screamed, wishing I could send even half of my headache into Richard's skull. When the magical flames hit Cassandra, they didn't roll over and engulf her son right away. Instead, that inferno stopped in its tracks for a count of three. Cosmo Gitano made it through my portal just before it snapped shut.

I blinked, wetting my cheeks. Cassandra had made the ultimate sacrifice for her son, but it shouldn't have worked. It truly had been too late. Only Gnomes could hold back time like that. I wracked my brain for any other explanation, gazing at the spot where the Psychic lay burning. Then I realized that time hadn't stopped. The magic had simply cut off the closer it got to me, like it had hit a wall at the last second.

"My portal." I blinked, knowing that I hadn't closed it. Someone from the other side had cut it off. I waved one hand and kept my mouth shut. My enemy didn't need to know that.

"Yes." I watched the Extramagus scoop the remaining eggshells into a glass vial. He waved a hand at them until they resembled metal filings, then tucked it in a pocket. "You opened it in the room of the queen's hostage. It proves you're a traitor to your court and monarch." Richard reached out with one hand, slapping something heavy around my wrists.

"I'm your prisoner, then." I closed my eyes, letting him drag me out the door alongside him.

"Yes. And I'll enjoy your execution immensely." His voice came soft and close, beside my left ear.

"I haven't been tried or sentenced yet." My retort sounded hollow and distant.

"When I rule, there will be no such nonsense for people like you."

I hoped with all my heart that someone—anyone—had overheard that remark. Richard Hopewell was more treacherous than I'd ever considered being.

Gemma

"Henny, thank the gods!" Hertha Harcourt leaped from the center of the brilliance, carrying a silvery bundle.

I shielded my eyes from the bright light that came with the unexpected voice in Henrietta Thurston's office, trying to see more.

"We need shadows so they can't see this side!" The headmistress sprang over the desk, tails streaming out behind her to help her stick the landing. "Close the portal as soon as they're through."

A soothing fog of indigo rolled in to dim things back down to levels resembling normal. One glance in its general direction confirmed that Maddie had cast an Umbral spell, her wand held under Henry Baxter's arm as he held his hands over his face.

"On it." I held out one hand, fighting with the opposing court's magic as I tried to knock it over. For a moment, I wondered why I had so much trouble, but then I saw who'd opened it. "Al?"

He didn't even glance in my direction, and I couldn't blame him. Richard Hopewell barged into the room Albert Dunstable stood in, his hands lit up with Fire and Spectral magic. Al stood his ground, along with an elderly woman and what looked like a half-spider, half-goblin man. I couldn't hear a word they said.

When Hopewell burned the old lady, Maddie screamed. She sent even more of her shadows in front of Henry, her magic taking on the shape of a kite shield, but Richard's flames never made it near the portal, even though a blast that big should have.

When the half-pint barged through, he ran right into me, but trolls like me are tough, so I didn't fall. He grabbed me around the waist, his shoulders hitching with sobs.

Al took one look over his shoulder and blinked, then waved one hand like an afterthought. As my magic snapped the portal shut, I watched Hopewell clap him in what passed for irons in the Under. I glanced around, trying to find Hope. She was supposed to be with him. The Redford kid, too, but the Klingon on my starboard bow wasn't the state's youngest medium.

"Who are you, and where's my daughter?" I pried the kid's hands off me and looked down into his face. I immediately felt like a heartless bitch.

It was frozen with grief. I wasn't sure he'd ever stop crying, not on the inside, anyway. The whys and wherefores weren't important, either, only that this poor child, who looked an awful lot like Tony Gitano once I thought about it, had some serious trauma to deal with in his near future.

"Miss Tolland." The simpering voice was a blast from my distant and recent past. "Gemma."

"Captain Tolland will do, Mrs. Harcourt." I turned my gaze on her, narrowing it until she appeared to be at the end of a tunnel. "Where is my daughter?"

"With mine." She laid a bundle of what looked like spider-shifter silk on the headmistress' desk. "In here."

"Are you kidding me?" I put one arm around the still-shuddering mystery boy because I didn't dare risk monarchical wrath descending on Hope's head by touching that cocoon.

"No." She shook her head. "Your, ah, um, ex-paramour got us out in the nick of time."

The bundle of silk shook, then pitched from left to right. Had it gotten bigger? Muffled voices came from inside it. The crying boy untangled himself from my side and jumped on the polished mahogany surface, tearing at strands like he was at the world's saddest birthday party.

The air cleared, brightening the room as the headmistress used her Air magic to remove smoke that had come through the portal with everyone else. Maddie recalled her shadows, then leaned against Henry. She sniffled, her tear-streaked face making me wonder exactly why she'd screamed.

"Who was she?" I asked the magus.

"Cassandra Spanos," Henry answered for his girlfriend. "She always had a kind word for Maddie last year, even though she couldn't remember her. She's been missing since last August, and we found out she gave loads of info to Hopewell."

"Except she didn't." The boy sat at the edge of the desk, hands covered in spider webs. He looked down. "My mom didn't tell them anything, except for the times that horrible man used mind magic to force predictions out of her."

"This is impossible." Maddie blinked. "Sandra's too young to have a kid your age. What are you? Nine? Ten?"

"I'm one. Almost. And the name's Cosmo."

"Nobu aged him, of course. His mother, too, the poor thing, but that's the price of assistance from a *Tsuchigomo*." Hertha Harcourt tied her hair into a knot on the top of her head, then went to work on the thick webbing Cosmo hadn't been able to tear through. She stopped, though, shaking her head. "Henny, hold this."

Hertha Harcourt slipped a jade dragon amulet over her head and held it out, but Henrietta Thurston didn't take it. The two women gazed at each other, the emotion between them nothing like what I'd seen when the headmistress had grieved for Neil with Henry.

"The only conclusion to draw now is that you've been helping my ex, Hertha. After everything we've been through together. I can't."

"Fine." I reached for it, but the dragon lady snatched it away.

"You must be crazy. This is a Seelie device." Hertha closed her eyes. "Henny. It's not me."

"I've got it." Henry stepped forward and grasped the chain, taking care not to put his hands on the business end of the arti-fact. He eyed it though, and I figured he'd touch it eventually.

"Thank you." Claws sprang from the ends of Mrs. Harcourt's fingertips and cut right through the cocoon still twined around the children. I made fists so tight that my nails cut into my hands. It should be me rescuing my daughter, faerie courts be damned, but at least Hertha was a mother. She'd be careful since her daughter was trussed up in there alongside mine.

An arm flopped out, longer than I expected, but the right shade and tone to be Hope's. A leg followed, half the calf revealed in what should have been ankle-length pants. Had they ridden up? The pit of my stomach dropped like I'd been tossed heaven-ward. No. My daughter had grown.

She slept, so her face wasn't too different, even with her cheeks less round than a kindergartner's typically were. But my little girl wasn't so little anymore, not when she could pass for a fourth-grader. According to Cosmo, she'd stepped up and saved a life. Hope was a full-fledged hero. The kid asleep on her chest proved it.

Her arms cradled an oversized dragon whelp, scales pale green with rounded ridges above her eyes instead of the wickedly sharp horns her mother sported when she shifted. Her tail had fins, not spikes. A water dragon, then. I'd never seen one in all my years at sea.

"They won't wake up just yet," said Henrietta. "We've got a

few minutes, at least. The *Tsuchigomo*'s magic took a lot out of them."

"You don't say." Hertha raised an eyebrow, then turned her gaze toward Henry. "Don't you have a memory charm or something that will tell us who the informant is?"

"I'm sorry for doubting you, Hertha." Henrietta pointed at a piece of paper floating in mid-air beside her. "This is Sir Dunstable's confession. It seems the queen ordered him to answer Richard's questions about us."

"And now he's Richard's prisoner." Hertha feigned a yawn. "Loose ends neatly tied. We don't have to lift a finger to see justice done."

"No." I put my hands on my hips. "You left it to me to rescue your son and his fiancée last spring, and let my daughter give years of her childhood for your baby just now. I've about had it with your every-dragon-for-herself attitude."

"And what are you going to do about it, troll?" Hertha bared her teeth, but I didn't let her get to me.

"What I should have done a long time ago." I reached into my coat and pulled my wand out of the inside pocket. Calling on my Air magic, I levitated the sleeping girls, binding them to my wand with a tether. "Rescue the people I love."

I turned on my heel and left, not caring which of them followed me, if any. Once I had the two kids settled in Maddie's dorm room, I headed for the one old Summoner who could get me directly into the queen's castle.

CHAPTER THIRTEEN

Albert

I stared at the round table's empty seat. Mine, usually. Fred sat in his, eyes burning with rage. I wondered who he was angrier at, Hopewell or me. Another blow fell across my back, still only the shaft of the cane. It hurt slightly less than the headache an Extramagus' proximity induced.

"You helped nocturnals. Unseelies."

"I helped my daughter." I swallowed a groan as he hit me again.

"She traded years to the *Tsuchigomo*. A traitor, like her father. When I see her again—"

"Enough, Richard." A long rustle of fabric told me Her Majesty had risen. "The child knew no better."

"Perhaps, Majesty. But the dragon did."

"Just so." Leather-soled slippers tapped across flagstones. The glimmering hem of Her Majesty's robes edged into the corners of my vision. "You will tell us where you sent Hertha Harcourt, as you've told us all about her son and his little friends. Speak the name of your portal's endpoint. Now."

"Newport."

"You lie." A third blow fell. This time, the shaft of Richard's cane crushed one of my ribs. "I felt the Unseelie magic."

"To Hope's mother." Closing my eyes, I swallowed a sob. I was too weak to protect the people I loved, one who truly needed it, and another who'd only just trusted me again. I was a failure, too weak. Again.

"You see now, my queen, that your knight is complicit with the king's people."

"Your Majesty," Fred's words came out strained.

"You may speak, Sir Redford."

"Sir Dunstable is not the only one of your knights with blood ties to the king's people. Will your prince say the same of me when my year and a day is up?"

"Unfortunate circumstances of birth and tithe have existed since the dawn of man, Majesty." The simper in Richard's voice made my blood boil.

"Incorrect." I tried like hell to push through pain and shame and channel Mr. Spock. "At the dawn of man, the unified courts meant Faerie did not contribute to that problem."

A whistle and a rush of air sounded above my head, and I shut my eyes against what might be the end but would certainly be more excruciating pain than my worst migraine ever. But the blow never fell. At least, not on me.

"Brodsky." Richard changed his cane's trajectory.

I looked up, not quite able to believe the old Summoner had the stones to show his face in the Seelie side of the Under, let alone the queen's castle. He'd been involved in undoing one of her punishments, after all. That blow from the cane toppled him, and he hit the flagstones with a sick snap and not even a single cry of pain. The old guy must have been through worse. Hadn't I heard he'd lived through ten years in a Siberian gulag? He passed out after that, the portal he'd opened fading along with his consciousness. But he hadn't come through alone.

"Gemma?" I shut my mouth, realizing that this was the second question I'd asked her on the same day.

"Watch it, Al."

"Destroy her!" The queen stepped between us, pointing one long, pale finger at the Unseelie troll captain who dared set foot in her throne room. Brownies like staves shot up from the cracks between flagstones, twisting to tether Gemma and bind her to the spot. She was a sitting duck.

"No." Richard extended one hand toward the queen. "I've got a better idea, Your Majesty."

Using his cane more as an accessory than something he needed to keep his balance, Richard Hopewell sauntered toward the western window. Facing the king's demesne, he called out a challenge, one his rank as prince empowered him to make.

The Extramagus, bolstered by almost the entire Seelie population, had made his move. If he won against the king, all restrictions on his magic in the mortal realm would vanish. He'd be a full monarch, even more powerful than the queen, and if he married her, he might as well rule the entire Under.

I watched the queen and her power-crazed consort step back up the dais and take their seats. Turning my head so I wouldn't have to look at them would have been a relief if that hadn't meant looking at Gemma, who was stuck in a tangle of brownies. I sighed, not willing to make any move to escape, even though I could have.

"Looks like you won't get that date, Al."

"This is enough, Gem." Tapping into the same Sidhe magic the queen had used to call up the brownies, I made one addition she wouldn't kill me on the spot for. Roses, orange-amber like Gemma's hair, budded and bloomed all around her. "It always was and ever will be."

"'Ever' might not be for much longer." She smiled. "And if literal flowery stuff like this was the only thing between us, Hope wouldn't exist. But meeting like this is not enough for me, not anymore. And I'm sorry."

"Why?" The energy between us grew as I asked her the third question. Neither of us mentioned it. There wasn't time.

"I should have fought harder for you that night you didn't show up. Should have known it was your family and not you."

"I blame your lack of a stylish vision-correction apparatus." I pointed at my glasses, where they stuck out of my pocket. "You know what they say about hindsight."

"Oh, by the way, you owe me now." Her smile shimmered like sunlight on the ocean.

"Yes. I know. So what'll it be?"

"Save the world." Those hazel eyes glowed with a purpose.

"You must think I'm something special." I shook my head.

"You're a rare breed." Gemma's mouth flattened in what I always thought of as her serious face. "Al, haven't you ever wondered why a guy with your pedigree needs glasses and gets magically-induced headaches?"

"Watch out, or you'll cancel that debt before I can pay it." I shut my eyes, digging through memories to try to figure out the sum of those particular parts. Revelation rose in my mind like the sun. "I have blanks in my memory, Gem."

"Great Garters! Henry. His mentor, maybe." She blinked. "That's what the headmistress meant by the right time."

"Memory Psychics."

"Yeah. You weren't supposed to know. I should have told you the second I got here. But Al, you're not just a Sidhe. You've got magus powers of the rarest kind."

"Silence!" One of the roses covered Gemma's mouth at Richard's command.

If I'd paid more attention in Magus Studies, I'd have known right away what she meant. Setting up a duel took time, so I thought I'd remember something before the duel could start. But Richard was too smart for that.

The cane struck my head, knocking my consciousness loose like a boxer's tooth.

Albert

I woke slowly to the scent and taste of salt. The grit against my face told me we'd moved out of the castle and to a beach. I sat up, not wanting to get sand in my eyes by opening them, but I couldn't brush it off. My hands hung bound behind my back, so I shook my head instead.

Once some sand fell off, I opened my eyes and looked around. I sat on the beach, up past the tide line. Gemma, still bound by Brownies and roses, sat sleeping nearby. The section of beach we occupied was right at the border between the Seelie and Unseelie demesnes, with a set of amber banners on our side and another of indigo on theirs.

A dueling square had already been marked out in the sand, its borders made of silk. Over my shoulder, I saw the queen's pavilion where a seat befitting her station sat beside another for Richard. On the other side, where the sand of the beach turned from gold to jet, the king had a similar setup, except he had only one chair.

Drums beat from somewhere in the woods on the king's side, and I watched, waiting as the Unseelie contingent emerged from the tree line. Duke Neil walked with Duke Ismail, their presences so imposing that I almost didn't notice Gee-Nome limping ahead and setting their slow pace. The dukes took positions at the two corners on the king's side of the dueling square.

I wondered who'd stand up for Richard. With less than two year's familiarity with the queen's court, I didn't think it likely anyone would volunteer to marshal the lists on his side, but I was wrong. One person stepped forward, taking the spot that'd be at his left, on the woodward side. My mother. She didn't even spare me a glance, and I could hardly blame her. I was a traitor twice over, after all.

A series of splashes came from the seaward side, where Ren Ichiro stood shifting from Selkie to human form. He wore a low-slung pair of surf shorts with a yellow and white Hawaiian print and approached the last empty corner without bothering to put on more suitable attire. He caught my eye and rolled his, confirming my suspicion that he'd offered to be there for some reason I couldn't fathom.

The royal entourages arrived, with high-ranking individuals in tow. It didn't much matter whether said beings were tithed fae, guests, or hostages like the *Tsuchigomo* who paced behind the queen, unbound even though he was her prisoner. Each person in attendance added to the figurative prestige and literal power on either side.

The king's people outnumbered the queen's, although his guests held power at lower levels on average to hers. Portals opened to admit more guests from the mortal realm. The reason Rhode Island was so important to the monarchs was that its contradictions somehow make an eclectic whole. It's one of the few places in the entire world where portals from both sides opened side by side. They were separate for each court but originated at the same location—in front of the monument at Swan Point Cemetery.

I saw Henrietta Thurston arrive on the queen's side, red ears poking out of her hair and tails to match trailing behind her. At her side walked Hertha Harcourt, the amulet keeping her in humanoid form. The dragon lady had two children in tow.

I realized one was Hope, although she'd grown at least five inches in height and aged by at least three years. She had one rainbow-hued wing around the other kid, a girl of about ten years. I did not recognize her at first. Her skin was so pale it was almost blue, and her hair was black with green highlights. When I noticed her wearing an amulet identical to Hertha's, I understood. This was Saya, the dragon child my daughter had rescued from the doom of premature birth.

Henrietta and Hertha stood near the pavilion but the two girls continued on, stopping in front of the queen's throne. Saya took a knee but Hope stood, chin tilted to look the Seelie monarch right in the eye.

"Your Majesty I, um, humbly request that you release my father and mother, so they can watch this duel just like your other guests."

"Your parents are my prisoners, child. Dangerous."

"And so is he, Your Majesty." Hope held out one hand to indicate the *Tsuchigomo*. "Yet Mister Nobu is allowed to attend unbound."

"Your argument is as impeccable as any of your grandmother's, young Alkonost." The queen tilted her head toward my mother, then nodded at Fred Redford.

With Richard off suiting up for his duel and not at her side to nay-say, I shouldn't have been surprised that Her Majesty granted Hope's request. The smile my daughter gave me as she curtsied her way out of the queen's immediate presence struck me harder than a blow to the chest. I'd been the one to coach her on courtly speech, and even though she'd declared the lessons boring, she'd absorbed them.

"You don't deserve this, but I'll do as Her Majesty bids." Fred's tone cut as deep as his blade through my bonds. With a whistle, he ordered away the brownies imprisoning Gemma.

"Nonetheless, thank you."

"You'd better have a damn good reason for breaking the rules, Al." Fred shook his head. The veneer of anger didn't quite hide a weariness I understood all too well. Playing both sides drained a person.

"From my point of view, it's a good reason. I won't presume to know yours. For the third time, thanks."

"Fine." Fred stepped back to his honor guard position near the pavilion.

"Redcaps." Gemma snorted.

"So I've learned." I shrugged. "Fred means well, and the strict rules of Seelie suit him. But the law here is hard."

"Tell me about it." She grinned. "This show's gonna go on no matter what we do."

"Yes." I smiled. "We should remain vigilant, as we've learned to do as a knight and a captain."

"Nah." Gemma chuckled. "We should remember our lessons better than that."

"So it's all of Faerie we're protecting, then?"

"And maybe the mortal world, too." She shrugged. "Same difference to us."

"Considering everything I've seen and heard about Richard Hopewell, you're right."

"You really know the way to a girl's heart." Gemma winked. "Telling her she's right and all."

"Not a girl, a woman. And of course, I know. I've loved you for what seems like forever."

"I never stopped, either. Loving you, I mean, Al."

"Then there's nothing we can't face, Gem."

"Not even if it ends in disaster?"

"Not even then."

And of course, it did.

CHAPTER FOURTEEN

Gemma

I watched the first group come in from the portal on the king's side. Henry Baxter escorted a spry older woman with Ed Redford in tow while Tony and Olivia trailed behind. The woman held one of those crocheted shopping bags with something inside. When she saw me, she tugged Tony's sleeve, then whispered in the black-furred ear he bent toward her.

Tony shook his head, then pointed to Ed. The woman sighed, her shoulders drooping like she'd rather go to bed than attend a duel. She reached into a pocket and handed something from it to the young medium. He stood staring into the trees, oblivious until she tapped him on the shoulder. He pointed at whatever he'd seen. Tony and Olivia both looked, and she put her hands over her mouth. He hung his head. I saw his lips form the name "Bianca."

Ed patted Tony's shoulder and left the group of them, his eyes on the ground. When he got near the boundary between the demesnes, a line of gnomes barred his way. The kid pointed at his brother, and the pint-sized faeries let him through. He made a beeline for us, but Fred stopped him.

Edward Redford was seated on the left side of the queen's pavilion next to Hope and her new dragon friend, clutching whatever trinket the lady gave him. His feet didn't touch the ground, but the two girls' did. The difference offered a stark reminder that my baby wasn't anything resembling one anymore.

Hope whispered something to Ed and he nodded, shivering even though it wasn't cold. She reached down and took his hand. Had I been the one who'd taught her to share courage with her friends and allies?

"You did right by her, Gem." I heard the smile in Al's voice and turned to look at him so I could see it with my eyes.

"Hope so."

"I should have been there."

"You will be now." I turned my hand palm up on my lap, offering it like Hope had, even though I knew he couldn't take it without getting us both killed. But even if you can't accept the invitation, sometimes just knowing you're welcome makes all the difference.

A blast of trumpets interrupted as the monarchs entered. The king strode out of thick underbrush that cut the beach off from the rest of the wild Unseelie woods. The queen waved at the neatly manicured topiary maze that bordered her side of the shore. Richard emerged, decked out in the typical Sidhe armor, which meant shiny and lightweight.

By contrast, the king wore his usual clothes. Usual, not regular. The Goblin King favored long coats and frilly shirts under tight doublets or vests. Nothing on his body looked like armor, but I knew he didn't need it. Goblins defended themselves by not getting hit.

While the king made his way down to the dueling square right away, Richard stopped and poured the queen a drink. As he prepared her cup, his body blocked the whole refreshment table from her view. I saw everything, though. Fine dust fell into the cup from his sleeve just before wine flowed like blood into the ivory vessel.

It looked accidental, but my gut told me it couldn't be. I made myself a promise to keep Her Majesty from drinking that concoction no matter what.

But the queen refused the beverage for the time being, setting it aside after her consort offered it. As Richard belted on his silver sword and dagger, he smiled with his mouth, although his eyes remained mirthless. He approached the square, staring daggers at the king.

Each of the combatants spoke with their marshals in hushed tones. I hadn't seen an actual formal duel like this before. Most of the lower-ranked fae had contests more closely resembled a pro wrestling match than anything else.

Richard tossed a glove into the square, then stepped over the ropes. The king nodded and entered from his side. They faced each other, the king saluting by placing one heart over his chest, but Richard refused to return the favor. Instead, he turned his head and spat on the sand.

Movement from the corner of my eye caught my attention like flame to a moth. The queen had reached for her goblet.

I stood and snatched it myself. Everyone stared.

"To Your Majesty's continued good health and well-being," I said.

I chugged.

"What was that, Captain Tolland?" Ed Redford tilted his head.

I mumbled something about the pirate code and sat back down, stomach churning. Nobody was paying any attention by that point.

Down the beach, the duel had begun.

Albert

The silver sword hung at the wrong angle in Richard Hopewell's hand, light glinting off it from all the wrong places as he held it in a novice's grip. I wondered at first what business he had on the inside of a dueling square, but then he busted out his magic.

The Goblin King leapt and dodged out of the way, as adept as any Olympic acrobat in the extrahuman category. I'd expected nothing less from a godlike being. Richard didn't land a blow, although he showed off an impressive array of magical schools. Ice rimed the stakes at the square's corners. Lightning made fulgurites on the sand in two tones. My head pounded like a wet towel hitting the back of my eyes.

I stood up, intending to move as far away as Sir Fred would allow. Instead of letting me go, Fred made me sit closer, next to his brother on the kids' bench.

"You need this, Al." Ed pressed something into my hand. I took it but couldn't look at it since I had to keep pretending to watch the duel. It felt like my head would shatter into a million pieces if I didn't.

But the many-pointed thing I held had other ideas. A different scene imposed itself on my field of vision, like when you're watching a movie and someone gets between you and the screen.

I saw myself at Trout Academy with Gemma in our freshman year. That wasn't any surprise, but being in the principal's office was. I had no memory of any disciplinary action against me back in high school, just waiting outside the office as Gemma endured hers.

"You understand, Mr. Dunstable, that the use of Null magic is banned at Trout." The old, bald man who spoke was not the principal, though he wore a rumpled suit and tie with his shabby Greek fisherman's cap. "They must promote a learning environment where magi can exercise their schools of magic without barriers. While here, you will stick strictly to your Sidhe powers. I hope I am making this clear."

"Abundantly, sir." I had my hands behind my back, held so tightly by tradition they could have as easily been tied with rope.

"But his headaches—"

"Miss Tolland, you're the one who encouraged him, so it will be you who helps him with his headaches. I understand that you have Air magic besides the skills that come with being a troll changeling."

"Gladly." Gemma gave me a look that melted me, both back in the memory and in the present. I thought I'd always loved her by some stroke of destiny, even before we'd met, but this was it. The missing memory had contained the moment her name etched itself on my heart.

"He will need to know someday, however. At the right time and no sooner." The man who wasn't the principal stepped forward, holding one hand out.

He pressed a medal against Gemma's forehead, then lifted it. Her eyes went blank, like she couldn't see or hear in the same time and place as me.

"Who are you?"

"Edgar Watkins." He sighed. "I'm sorry to do this to you, but Joyce will use this memory to save the world years from now. You're Null, which means you can cancel any magic, and as soon as you remember this day, you must do it in a big way. We don't know the exact ending for you two," he glanced at Gemma, "but I sincerely hope it's the happiest possible."

"Hope," Gemma said. After that, Edgar Watkins touched the medal to my head, and the scene ended.

The next thing I saw was Richard on the run from the king's attack. He dragged the sword behind him like he had no idea what to do with it. The silver glint had gone dull, and I sensed a new aspect to my headache. Richard Hopewell had used Earth magic, which affected metals. He'd turned that silver blade to iron.

"I know what I have to do now." I stood again.

"Oh no, you don't." Fred reached out, trying to stop me. I threw the memory medal at him. When he caught it, he froze, paralyzed by whatever it had to show him.

I called on all the extra speed my Sidhe powers offered, stopping in a skid just short of crossing the square's ropes.

Focusing my eyes and that blinding headache on the sword in Richard's hands, I unleashed all my pain on it, hoping that was the energy needed to cancel the king-killing spell.

Instead of deadly iron, a silver sword scraped the king's side, and Richard screamed his rage. The sword and the dagger dropped in the sand. Empty hands pointed my way, and he proceeded to hurl every form of magic he possibly could at me, forfeiting the match.

Within inches, every single one of his attacks fizzled out. The marshals called the duel and the queen's voice rang in my ears, stripping Richard of his rank and rejecting his tithe. He roared with anger, flinging out one hand to open a portal back to Swan Point.

Tony and Olivia stood shoulder to shoulder, holding hands as they pointed together at the weakening wall between worlds. I saw Lane and Margot on the other side, standing in the cemetery in a pose mirroring the shifters. The others were there, too, everyone from PPC Richard had failed to defeat. Bobby and Lynn, Henry and Maddie, Josh and Nox, Blaine and Kim. Jeannie stood with them, although Ismail winked from his corner of the dueling square. Beth Dennison stood, arms crossed as she nodded at Ren. Irina Kazynski waved to Fred and Ed.

They'd assembled to reinforce coincidence and ensure Richard's failure. The sight of them made him clench his fists, face red and blotchy. He lunged forward, probably trying to get far enough away from my Null magic to sling spells at them as he escaped the Under. But they vanished just before Hopewell jumped through, replaced by a desk, filing cabinets, and people in suits.

The Extramagus had landed inside an FBE office somewhere near Washington, DC. Without his faerie magic, he had nothing to fight with but his fists.

My head felt light and painless, his magic cutting out completely even through that open portal. Gino Gitano stood flanked by guards, laughing in an orange jumpsuit. Derek Dennison grinned at us, waving as his partner Natalie slapped cuffs on Hopewell. The way closed. We'd defeated him without breaking any faerie laws.

I opened my mouth, but the cheer died in my throat. Hope called out for her mama. When I turned back toward the queen's pavilion, Gemma had fallen.

CHAPTER FIFTEEN

Gemma

By the time Al got down to the dueling square, I knew exactly what Richard had intended to poison the queen with—iron shavings. Trolls have a superior constitution to Sidhe, but it was killing me, anyway.

With one hand over my gut, I tried to get away long enough to try to discreetly sick it up, uncertain it'd make one bit of difference. Every move took more effort. I felt heavy, like my arms and legs had doubled their weight. Iron is the heaviest metal.

I got exactly four steps away from the bench I'd sat on. After that, my body gave up. That was the strangest thing for someone like me, who relied on the extra strength from my faerie side.

Trying to sit was an abject failure. Instead, I toppled over. My face went hot, and probably red too. Iron, embarrassment, or the two combined; it didn't matter. Inside my belly, a million claws tore at my guts. I was dying.

"Mama!" Hope fled to my side, kneeling close but not touching. "Mama, your skin's covered with iron sores. Are you all right?"

"I'll get better in a minute, baby." I swallowed the truth but couldn't stop my tears. I would have closed my eyes to keep them in, but I didn't want to lose sight of my little girl.

"If I have anything to do with it, she will." Al stood over us, his hair unkempt and windblown, his stance victorious.

"You beat him? Richard?"

"Not just me. Everyone—all our friends. He's not a problem anymore, Gem."

"We saved the worlds then?" I winced. My whole body burned with the iron in my bloodstream.

"Stop. You already owe me back."

"I'll never stop, Al. Not even when I'm gone. I'll haunt you. Didn't I make that clear?" I held up one hand, gazed at the iron-induced blemishes. They looked like blistering burns shot through with rusty flecks.

"Yeah, you did."

"Gone?" Hope reached out a hand, about to touch me. I didn't have the strength to flinch away or stop her.

"No, kiddo." Al hugged our daughter close, then set her back on the bench I'd collapsed behind. "I've got an old promise to keep."

And then he held his hands over mine, not touching me with anything but the anti-magical energy coming from them. The pain vanished. The sores did, too. At first, I didn't understand. No faerie or magus power could reverse injury. Only shifters had rapid regeneration, and that was an individual ability. They couldn't use it on someone else.

"How?"

"Null magic, Gem." He moved his hands up, hovering them over my arms to erase the damage the poison had done to them. "But there's a price."

"Iron isn't magical, though. How are you doing this?"

"It's not the metal I'm nullifying, Gemma, it's the part of you that makes it deadly. I'm so sorry."

"Don't apologize, just don't stop." My tears dried. "I only want to live and raise our daughter."

By then, I didn't care what magic he eradicated. The sores had vanished from my hands, but so had the thick troll claws I sported in the Under. My muscles thinned, and I would have gotten weaker if the iron hadn't already done that number on my body.

As the soothing absence of pain spread along my extremities, I noticed Al's hair. Had it changed color? Gone to the honey blond it appeared to be in the mortal realm instead of the Under's Sidhe-alabaster? And was he squinting, like he always did outside the Under when he needed his glasses?

"You're tearing our magic away. All of it."

"Yes and no." Al leaned over, gazing into my eyes. "Only most of it."

My body felt much better, except for my stomach and head. Was that what migraines felt like? The pain behind my eyes got intense enough for me to firmly believe that Albert Dunstable was the most courageous man in the known universe. If he'd functioned with pain like that for most of his life, he had a will of steel.

"It's not leaving, not all the way." I coughed.

"I think I know how to fix that, Gem." He leaned closer. "If it's okay?"

He put his lips to mine, not quite touching, as though asking permission. I lifted my arms, one to his shoulder and the other around his neck as I'd done all those years ago, and accepted his kiss. I had to hope that with the Null force removing our faerie natures, the tithes wouldn't turn our embrace into a death sentence.

When we broke away, a rush of sound met our ears, rising in volume above the ocean waves. I looked up, finally free from pain and unburdened. The smiles surrounding us were like rows of stars, shining down their approval.

Hope and the other children held hands, cheering. Fred slapped his hands together, blushing almost as deep a crimson as the cap on his head. The *Tsuchigomo* applauded with his hands and two pairs of his feet. Even Hertha Harcourt spared us a grin with her golf-clap.

"Enough!" The queen's voice rang like steel on bone.

"No, it's not." The king stepped through the crowd, pushing between Hertha and the *Tsuchigomo*. He held a wooden box, ornately carved.

"Get back on your side, Baelgreth, or so help me—"

"That's what I'm here to do, Illyana. Help." The king extended his hand. Al took it and rose, then helped me to my feet.

"You help my prisoners—transgressors in my demesne—yet my one request of you, ages ago, you denied me."

"My greatest mistake. I find these rebels of yours inspiring."

"They're inspiring me to new heights of anger."

"I can't blame you." The king took a knee before his former wife.

"You're mad, Baelgreth."

"Love is like madness at times." He opened the box and presented it to her, revealing something dainty that shone brightly in the sunlight. "Marry me, Illyana. Again. Please."

"Déjà vu." I rubbed my temples. Maybe it was the strange lightness of being unburdened by the ties of my tithe that caused me to continue, "You know, when he asked, I said yes. Sometimes you just have to admit that you want a second chance and damn the torpedoes."

"Your former captain has an unhindered tongue." The queen looked down her nose at the king, not giving me a second glance. "I wonder why she believes it is her place to speak on this matter, or to me?"

"Begging Your Majesty's pardon, but she did save your life by drinking the poisoned cup." Al slid his glasses over his rounded ears. "Our laws are clear on lives owed."

"They're hardly your laws now, Null magus." The queen tilted her head at Al. "But you are correct. The Air magus may address me."

"I hope my words will help you steer your course, Your Majesty."

"If only I were certain that Baelgreth is sincere." She gazed out at the sea.

"There's never any way to know that for sure, Majesty." I held my hands out. Albert took my left hand and our daughter rushed to my side to clasp my right. "The best you get is hope."

"It's enough for me, Illyana." The king's eyes plead in shades of melting amber. "I swear that this time, we can build a real family. If a knight and a pirate can work things out, even under the burdens we each placed on their shoulders, why can't we?"

His question took her breath away. The two monarchs eyed my little family with something more akin to longing than envy. When their eyes met again, the air quivered with promise. The rest of the crowd gasped their astonishment like fish out of water when the queen nodded and let the king slip the ring on her finger. But our little family didn't.

We knew all about hope and second chances after all.

The End

Have you started D.R. Perry's latest series, *Gallows Hill Academy?*

Available at Amazon and Kindle Unlimited.

Free bird? Don't make me laugh.

I'm Mavis Merlini and I want out. Of my shady family, this rowdy school, maybe even the world.

My brother got kicked out of Gallows Hill School for inciting mermaid violence. I'm determined to cut out all distractions and be the first of my six siblings to actually graduate. Which means living on campus and ignoring my extroverted roommate.

All my plans are doomed to failure when a goth lion shifter in a trench coat drops his feather. Of course I pick it up. It's shiny and I'm a raven shifter. I swear I meant to give it back. But now it's magically bonded to me and I can't. Now I've got obligations to a Faerie Monarch on top of everything else. And if I shirk them, I'll spend a hundred years in his dungeon.

Can I soar through this double life, or will I end up failing to launch?

Scroll up and click '**Buy Now**' or '**Read for Free**' to join the adventure with Mavis and friends!

Get your copy today!

CONNECT WITH THE AUTHOR

Find D.R. Perry Online

Website: https://drperryauthor.com/

Author Central: http://www.amazon.com/-/e/B00O6851HO

Facebook: https://www.facebook.com/drpperry/

Mailing List: https://app.mailerlite.com/webforms/landing/p9i8u6

Twitter: https://twitter.com/DRPerry22